HER CHRISTMAS GUARDIAN

SHIRLEE MCCOY

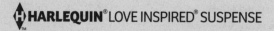

Recycling programs for this product may not exist in your area.

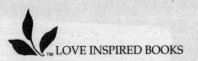 LOVE INSPIRED BOOKS

ISBN-13: 978-0-373-44636-0

Her Christmas Guardian

www.Harlequin.com

Printed in U.S.A.

"Shhhhh," Boone said. "You're okay."

"No. It's not," Scout sobbed. "Lucy is missing."

"I didn't say it was okay. I said *you* were." He eased back, cupping her face in his hands, his eyes dark blue and filled with compassion. "There's a big difference, Scout. One you have no control over. The other you do."

"I don't have any control over any of it, that's the problem." She stepped away, swiping at the tears.

"You know what I've realized during the years my daughter's been missing?" he asked quietly, his hair gleaming in the afternoon sunlight, his eyes deeply shadowed. "We don't always have to be in control to be content. We don't always have to know every outcome to have peace."

Coming from anyone else, it would have sounded trite, but Boone had lived her nightmare. He knew every ache of her heart.

"I wish I had your faith. I wish that I could believe something good was going to come out of this."

"I wish I had my daughter. But, I don't, and because I don't, I'm helping you find yours."

Books by Shirlee McCoy

Love Inspired Suspense

Die Before Nightfall
Even in the Darkness
When Silence Falls
Little Girl Lost
Valley of Shadows
Stranger in the Shadows
Missing Persons
Lakeview Protector
*The Guardian's Mission
*The Protector's Promise
Cold Case Murder
*The Defender's Duty
†Running for Cover
Deadly Vows
†Running Scared
†Running Blind
Out of Time
†Lone Defender

†Private Eye Protector
  The Lawman's Legacy
†Undercover Bodyguard
†Navy SEAL Rescuer
  Tracking Justice
†Fugitive
†Defender for Hire
  Texas K-9 Unit Christmas
    "Holiday Hero"
  Safe by the Marshal's Side
**Protective Instincts
**Her Christmas Guardian

Love Inspired Single Title

  Still Waters

*The Sinclair Brothers
†Heroes for Hire
**Mission: Rescue

SHIRLEE McCOY

has always loved making up stories. As a child, she daydreamed about elaborate tales in which she was the heroine—gutsy, strong and invincible. Though she soon grew out of her superhero fantasies, her love for storytelling never diminished. She knew early that she wanted to write inspirational fiction, and she began writing her first novel when she was a teenager. Still, it wasn't until her third son was born that she truly began pursuing her dream of being published. Three years later, she sold her first book. Now a busy mother of five, Shirlee is a homeschooling mom by day and an inspirational author by night. She and her husband and children live in the Pacific Northwest and share their house with a dog, two cats and a bird. You can visit her website, www.shirleemccoy.com, or email her at shirlee@shirleemccoy.com.

Here is what I am commanding you to do.
Be strong and brave. Do not be terrified.
Do not lose hope. I am the Lord your God.
I will be with you everywhere you go.
—*Joshua* 1:9

To Beth.
I miss going on long walks with you and your kids!

ONE

I've been found.

The thought shot through Scout Cramer's head, left her breathless, frantic. She veered the shopping cart toward the store exit, her heart pounding, her body vibrating with fear.

In her periphery, a man moved in. Casual in his dark slacks and sport coat, he looked like any other holiday shopper. She wanted so badly to believe he was.

Please, God. Please. Let me be wrong about who he is.

But she didn't think she was.

She thought she was right. Thought that somehow, after nearly three years, everything she'd tried to do for Amber, everything she'd tried to do for herself and Lucy had come to nothing. *If* she'd been found out, *if* he'd learned the truth, it was all for nothing. Every lie. Every broken friendship.

All of it.

For nothing.

"Please, God," she whispered as she unhooked Lucy's belt and lifted her from the cart. At just a little over twenty-four pounds, she was tiny for her age, her little arms wrapping snugly around Scout's neck.

"Mommy needs to find the restroom," Scout murmured, afraid to walk out into the parking lot. He'd follow her there. She was sure of it. After that…

What would he do?

Confront her?

Worse?

The store was filled with holiday shoppers, dozens of people crowding into Walmart's long lines, all of them desperate for Christmas bargains.

Would anyone notice if Scout was attacked?

Would anyone intervene?

Maybe, but she didn't plan to stick around long enough to find out.

She glanced at the man, hoping he didn't notice her sideways look. He was still, hovering at the head of an aisle, pretending to look at cans of asparagus.

She pivoted away, hurrying toward a restroom sign and the corridor beyond it. There had to be an emergency exit. She nearly ran to the end of the hall, stopping at double doors marked Employees Only.

What would happen if she walked in?

Would someone call the police? Set off an alarm?

Would she be arrested? If she was, what would happen to Lucy?

She looked at her little girl, smiling into dark brown eyes that were so much like Amber's it hurt to look in them.

"It's going to be okay," she whispered, and she hoped she was right. She'd made a lot of mistakes in her life. She'd done a lot of things she'd regretted, but she'd never regretted her friendship with Amber. She'd never regretted the promise she'd made to her.

Even if she did sometimes wonder if she'd been right to make it.

She glanced over her shoulder. No sign of the guy in the sport jacket. But her skin crawled, and her hair stood on end.

Something wasn't right, and that scared her more than anything else that had happened in the past couple of years.

She pushed the door open, took a step into what must have been an employee break room. No one there. Thank goodness. Just vending machines, a microwave, a refrigerator. Straight across from where she stood, an external door with a small window offered the hope of escape she'd been looking for.

"Everything okay, ma'am?" The voice was so unexpected, she jumped, whirling to face the speaker, her heart in her throat, her arms tightening around Lucy.

Tall.

That was the first impression she got.

Very tall, because she was eye to chest, staring straight at a black wool coat that hung open to reveal a dark purple dress shirt.

She looked up into ocean-blue eyes and a hard, handsome face, took in the black knit cap that almost covered deep red hair, the auburn stubble, the deep circles beneath the man's eyes. He smiled, and his face changed. Not hard any longer. Approachable. The kind of guy a woman might put her trust in.

If she ever put her trust in anyone.

"I'm fine," she managed to say.

"You're in the employee break room," he pointed out,

flashing an easy smile. There was nothing easy about the look in his eyes. She was being studied, assessed, filed away for future reference.

"Yes. Well." She glanced around, trying to think of a good excuse for being in a place she shouldn't be. "I was looking for the restroom."

"You passed it."

"I guess I did." Her cheeks heated, but she refused to look away. He hadn't hauled out handcuffs or threatened to arrest her yet, so he probably wasn't a security guard or police officer. She doubted he was working with the man who'd been following her. She'd have noticed him way before she'd noticed the other guy. That dark red hair and lanky height weren't easy to miss. "I'll just go find it."

She sidled past him, moving back into the hall, Lucy's arms still tight around her neck. She'd do anything for her daughter. *Anything.* Even run away from everything she knew. Give up a job she loved. Say goodbye to friends and never contact them again.

"Are you in some kind of trouble?" the guy asked, following her down the hall.

Was she?

She didn't know, wasn't made for intrigue and danger. She liked quiet predictability. No drama. No muss. Nothing that was even close to trouble. The one time she'd tried to break free, do something wild and reckless and completely different, she'd caused herself enough heartache to last a lifetime.

No more.

Never again.

Except that she *had* done it again. Gone out on a limb, done something completely out of character. For different reasons, but the results had been the same. Trouble. It was breathing down her neck. She felt it as surely as she felt Lucy's soft breath on her cheek.

"Ma'am?" The man touched her arm, and she jerked back, surprised and a little alarmed. She'd kept mostly to herself since moving to River Valley, Maryland, spent all her time with Lucy or at work. She didn't let people into their world, into the place she'd carved for them. The safe little house in the safe little neighborhood.

"*Are* you in trouble?" he asked again, shoving his hands in the pockets of his black slacks and taking a step back.

"No," she mumbled even though she wasn't sure. The guy in the sport jacket seemed to have disappeared, and she was beginning to think she'd let her imagination get the better of her. But if she hadn't…?

Then what?

Could she run again?

Did she need to?

"Sure looks like you are to me."

"I'm fine," she insisted, and he nodded solemnly, his blue eyes never leaving her face.

"I'm glad to hear it, ma'am, but just in case you decide you're not—" he pulled a wallet out of his pocket, took a business card from it "—take this. I can help. If you decide you need it."

She took the card. Plain white with black letters and a small blue heart in one corner. "'Daniel Boone Anderson. Hostage Rescue and Extraction Team,'" she read out loud.

He nodded. "That's right."

"I'm not a hostage." She tried to give the card back, but he shoved his hands in his pockets, still eyeing her solemnly.

"That doesn't mean you don't need rescuing," he responded.

"I—"

"Take care of yourself and that baby." He nodded, one quick tilt of his head, and walked off, long legs eating up the ground so quickly he was out of the corridor and around the corner before she could blink.

She shoved the card in her coat pocket.

She wouldn't use it. Couldn't.

She'd promised Amber that she wouldn't tell anyone the truth about Lucy. She'd promised that no matter what happened, she'd keep it to herself. At the time, she'd expected Amber to be around, to help her navigate the world of subterfuge she'd agreed to. The fact that she wasn't didn't change the promise. Scout had an obligation to her friend. Even if she didn't, she had an obligation to herself and to Lucy. She couldn't cower in a store corridor, praying for rescue. She had to take action, do what needed to be done. Face her fear or call for help. One way or another, she needed to get moving.

"Mama! Go!" Lucy cried, impatient, it seemed, with staying in one spot.

"Okay, sweetie. I hear you." She put her shoulders back and her chin up, marched back to the break room as if she owned the place. Walked through the room as if she had every right to be there. Out the door and into the cold November evening. She'd parked close to the store entrance, and she had to walk around the side of the building to get there. Her heart tripped and jumped, the leaves rustling in the trees that lined the parking lot. A shadow moved in her periphery, and she took off, Lucy bouncing on her hip, giggling wildly as they rounded the side of the building.

* * *

The baby was giggling, but the woman looked scared out of her mind. Not that it was any of Daniel Boone Anderson's business. He should have gone back to hunting for the ingredients for pumpkin bread instead of leaving the store and waiting by the employee entrance. The problem was, he hadn't been too into the holidays during the past few years, and the entire store was decked out with tinsel and Christmas trees and wrapping paper. Every aisle had some reminder of the holiday he least liked to celebrate. The best Christmas had been the one right after Kendal's birth. Two months before Lana had walked out and taken their daughter with her.

Not Lana. He could almost hear his deceased wife's voice. *The Prophetess Sari. It has been ordained and it will be so.*

That had been her mantra when she'd finally contacted him. *Six months* after he'd returned from Iraq and found their empty apartment—and the note.

But he tried really hard not to think about that.

Four years was a long time to be missing a piece of your heart.

Which was probably why he spent so much time sticking his nose into other people's business and dealing with other people's problems.

He followed the woman around the side of the building, hanging back as she walked to an old station wagon. Nothing fancy, but she didn't seem like the fancy kind. Her jeans were a little too long, their scuffed cuffs dragging along the pavement as she buckled her daughter into a car seat. A long braid hung to the middle of her back. That had been what he'd noticed first—that long fall of golden-blond hair. Then he'd noticed the dark-haired little girl with her dimples and curls. Probably a couple of years younger than Kendal.

She'd turned five a couple of weeks ago.

He imagined her hair had grown long. It was probably straight as a stick, too.

But that was another direction he couldn't let himself go.

All the begging, all the searching, all the resources that were available, and he still hadn't been able to find Kendal. She'd been lost to someone in the cult. Probably someone who'd left it. Knowing Lana, she'd handed their daughter off without a second thought as to the child's welfare.

Boone never stopped thinking about it.

Even in his sleep, he dreamed about his daughter.

He clenched his fist, leaned his shoulder against a brick pillar that supported a narrow portico. Christmas shoppers moved past, hurrying into the store for whatever deal they thought Friday shopping would bring.

He noticed them, tracking their movements in the part of his brain that had been honed by years working long hours deep in enemy territory, but his focus was on the woman and her child. She opened the driver's door, tossed her purse into the vehicle, glanced around as if she was looking for someone.

Maybe whoever she was running from.

He was sure she was running. He'd seen it in her eyes when she'd lifted her daughter from the grocery cart and run toward the restroom—fear, desperation, all the things he saw in the gazes of the people he was hired to rescue.

The station wagon's headlights went on, and the woman backed out of the space. He'd have been wise to let her go and let the whole matter drop, but he'd never been all that wise when it came to things like this.

As a matter of fact, he often got himself in way deeper than he should be. Mostly because the one thing he wanted to accomplish, he hadn't been able to. He couldn't help himself, but he could help others.

Maybe he really did have an overinflated hero syndrome. That was what his coworker Stella said. She also said it was going to get him killed one day. She might be right about that, too, but he'd rather die trying to help someone than live knowing he hadn't.

He waited, watching as the woman drove to the edge of the parking lot. That should have been it—her driving out, Boone walking back into the store and retrieving the cart full of stuff that he'd left in aisle one.

Lights flashed near the edge of the parking lot. A hundred yards away, another set of headlights went on. A third followed, this one even closer to the exit the woman had used.

His heart jumped, adrenaline pumping through him, thoughts flooding in so quickly, he barely had time to process them before he was sprinting across the parking lot. Jumping into his SUV. All three cars were already exiting, and he had to wait for an elderly woman to make her way across the parking lot in front of him.

He made it to the exit as the last car turned east, its taillights disappearing from view. He followed, turning onto a narrow two-lane road that meandered through hilly farmland. A quiet road, nearly empty. Which wasn't good. His car would be easy enough to spot. Whether or not the guy in front of him realized he was being tailed depended on who was in the car.

They were making quite a line. His car, the one in

front and two more just ahead of it. Taillights about a quarter mile ahead that he was sure belonged to the woman's station wagon. He wasn't sure where they were heading, but he pulled out his cell phone. One thing he'd learned a long time ago—only a fool headed into trouble without backup.

He never had a chance to call for it. One minute, he was keeping his distance, watching the procession of cars. The next, the car in front of him braked hard. He had a split second to realize what was happening before his windshield exploded, bits of glass flying into his face and dropping onto the dashboard.

He accelerated, adrenaline surging, every cell, every nerve alert.

The next shot took out a front tire. The SUV swerved, sideswiping a tree and nearly taking out a stop sign. He fought for control, yanking the vehicle back onto the road, the ruined tired thumping, the procession of cars pulling farther ahead.

"Not good!" he muttered, the SUV protesting as he tried to pick up speed again.

Not going to happen. The bumpy road and the flat tire weren't a good combination. He jumped out of the SUV, glad he was carrying. He'd been known to leave his Glock at home. Carrying it around made him feel safe, but it also reminded him of loss and heartache. Of a hundred things that he was better off forgetting.

He snagged his cell phone, dialing Jackson's number, hoping that his friend would pick up. In all the years he'd known the guy, there'd been only a handful of times when he hadn't been available.

But then, that was the way the entire team was. There wasn't a member of HEART who wouldn't be willing to drop anything, travel any distance, risk whatever was necessary to help a comrade.

Jackson answered on the second ring. "Hello?"

"It's Boone."

"Yeah. I saw the number," Jackson said drily. "What's up?"

"I need your help."

"With?"

"I've got a situation."

"What kind of situation?" Jackson's tone changed, his words hard-edged and sharp.

"The kind that involves guns and bullets. A woman. A kid. Three cars that are following her," he responded.

"You call the police yet?"

"Probably would have been a good idea, but I'm not used to having police to rely on." He was used to being deep in a foreign country, working in places where the only people he could count on were his team members.

"Where are you?"

"I didn't see the name of the road. It's the first right north of the Walmart you brought me to a few days ago."

"I'll be there in ten."

"Call the police before you leave. I think we're going to—"

The sound of screeching tires split the quiet, and he shoved the phone back into his pocket, racing toward the sound. He'd covered a hundred yards when light burst to life in the distance.

Fire!

His heart jumped, the new surge of adrenaline giving wings to his feet. He sprinted toward the soft glow and the velvety black of the eastern sky, the sound of sirens splitting the night.

TWO

Get out! Get out, get out!

The words raced through Scout's mind as she crawled over the bucket seat and unbuckled Lucy's car seat. Black smoke filled the car, filled her lungs. She grabbed the seat, relieved that Lucy was babbling away, more excited, it seemed, than frightened by the crash, the smoke, the crackling fire.

Get out!

She reached for the door handle, coughing, gagging on blood that rolled from a cut on her forehead to the corner of her mouth.

The door flew open, and hands reached in, dragged her out, Lucy in the car seat, singing in that baby language that only a mother ever really understood.

Scout jerked away, the car seat slamming against her legs as she ran. Straight toward the black car that had been following her. She veered to the left, saw him. Just standing there. Sport coat and slacks, hands in his pockets. He could have been anyone, but she knew he was death coming to call.

"Who are you?" she rasped, backing toward the tree her car had run into when the tire was shot out.

"It really doesn't matter," he responded, pulling a cigarette from his pocket and lighting it. The cold calculation in his eyes made her blood freeze in her veins. She wanted to scream and scream and scream, but there was no one around to hear. Nothing that she could do but try to find a way out, pray that the police came quickly. Keep Lucy safe.

Please, God. Help me keep her safe.

"I called the police," she said, her heart pounding in her throat, her eyes burning from smoke and fear. Every nightmare she'd ever had was coming true. All the fear she'd lived with since she'd left San Jose congealed in the pit of her stomach, filled her with stark hard-edged terror.

She needed to think, to run, to do something to save her daughter.

That was all she knew. All she cared about.

She lifted the car seat higher, pulling it to her chest, the heavy ungainly plastic filled with the only thing she cared about. "They'll be here any minute," she continued, because he was staring at her, the cigarette dangling from his mouth. He must think he had all the time in the world, must believe that there was no way help could come in time.

God, please! She begged silently, easing toward the line of trees that had stopped the wagon from careening down an embankment.

She just had to make it into the trees, find someplace to hide.

The faint sound of sirens drifted on the cold November air. Her heart jumped; hope surged. She could do this. Had to do this. She ran into the trees, blood still sliding down her face, Lucy giggling as the car seat bounced. She had no idea. None.

Scout's feet slipped on slick leaves, and she went down hard, her hip knocking an overturned tree. She bounced back up, the car seat locked in her arms, Lucy now crying in fear, sirens growing louder.

"Sorry, but this just isn't your night." The words whispered from behind her, the cold chill of them shooting up her spine.

And suddenly, she wasn't alone with the man and his cigarette. Two dark shadows moved in, and she was fighting off hands that were trying to rip Lucy away from her.

She screamed as something slammed into her cheek. Heard Lucy's desperate cries and the sirens endlessly blaring. Heard her own frantic breathing and hoarse shouts.

A car door slammed and someone called a warning. To her? To the men who were attacking her? The car seat was ripped from her arms and something smashed into her temple. Darkness edged in, sprinkled with a million glittering stars.

She fought it, fought the hands that were suddenly on her throat. Lucy! She tried to cry, but she had no air for the words, no air at all.

She twisted, kneeing her attacker in the thigh.

Something flashed in the air near her head.

A gun?

She had only a moment to realize it, and then the world exploded, all the stars fading until there was nothing but endless night and the sound of her daughter's cries.

* * *

"Go after the car!" Boone shouted as he jumped from Jackson's car. "I'll check to see if there are any injuries."

Too late.

Those were the words that were running through his head over and over again.

Too late. Just as he'd been the day he'd arrived home from Iraq, ready to confront Lana about her prescription-drug problem, willing to work on their marriage so that they could make a good life for their child.

Too late.

He heard Jackson's tires screech, knew he'd taken off, following the car they'd seen speeding away. Dark-colored. A Honda, maybe. Jackson knew more about cars than he did, and he'd know the model and make.

Good information for the police, but none of it would matter if the woman and her daughter were hurt. Or worse.

He ran to the station wagon, ignoring the flames that were lapping out from beneath the hood. The back door was open, and he glanced in. No car seat. No child. No woman.

He checked the third-row bucket seat, then peered into the front. A purse lay on the passenger seat, and he snagged it, backing away from the burning vehicle. He doubted it would explode, but getting himself blown up wasn't going to help the woman, her kid or him.

He broke every rule his boss, Chance Miller, had written in the fifty-page HEART team handbook and opened the purse, pulling out the ID and calling Jackson with information on the woman. Scout Cramer. Twenty-seven. Five foot two inches. One hundred pounds. Organ donor. Blond hair. Blue eyes.

Victim.

He hated that word.

In a perfect world, there would be no victims. No losses. No hurting people praying desperately that their loved ones would return home.

Too bad it wasn't a perfect world.

He stepped away from the station wagon as a police cruiser pulled off the road. An officer ran to the back of the cruiser and dragged a fire extinguisher from the trunk.

Seconds later, the fire was out, the cold air filled with the harsh scent of chemicals and burning wires. Smoke and steam wafted from the hood of the car, but the night had gone quiet, the rustling leaves of nearby trees the only sound.

The officer approached, offering a hand and a quick nod. "Officer Jet Lamar. River Valley Police Department. Did you see what happened here?"

"I got here after the crash. I did see the woman and child who were in the car. They left the Walmart about fifteen minutes ago." And he didn't want to spend a whole lot of time discussing it. Scout and her daughter had disappeared. The more time that passed before they were found, the less likely it was that they ever would be.

Something else he had learned the hard way.

Every second counted when it came to tracking someone down.

"So, we've got two people missing?"

"Yes," Boone ground out. "And if we don't start looking, they may be missing for good."

"Other cars are responding. We have patrol cars heading in from the east. I just need to confirm that we're looking for a new-model Honda Accord. Dark blue."

Jackson must have provided that information, and Boone wasn't going to argue with it. He knew his friend well enough to know that he'd have to have been 100 percent sure before offering information. "That's right. It was pulling away as my friend and I arrived."

"I don't suppose you want to explain what you and your friend were doing on this road?" Officer Lamar looked up from a notepad he was scribbling in. The guy looked to be a few years older than Boone. Maybe closing in on forty. Haggard face. Dark eyes. Obviously suspicious.

"I followed the woman from Walmart. She looked like she might be in trouble."

"So, you just stepped in and ran to the rescue? Didn't think about calling the police?"

"I didn't want to call in the police over an assumption."

"Assumptions are just as often on target as they are off it. Next time," he said calmly, "call."

Boone didn't bother responding, just waited while Officer Lamar jotted a few notes, his gaze settling on the purse Boone still held.

"That belong to the victim?"

"Yes." Boone handed it over, shifting impatiently. "They could be across state lines by now."

"Not likely. We're about a hundred miles from the Penn state border. I'm going to take a look around. How about you wait in the cruiser?"

It wasn't a suggestion, but Boone didn't take orders from anyone but his boss or the team leader. He followed Lamar to the still-smoking station wagon, paced around the vehicle while Lamar looked in the front seat, turned on a flashlight and searched the ground near the car.

He didn't speak, but Boone could clearly see footprints in the moist earth near the car. Two sets. A woman's sneaker and a man's boot. "Looks like she survived the initial impact," Lamar murmured. He called something in on his radio, but Boone was focused on the prints—the deep imprint of the man's feet. The more shallow print of the woman's. There had to be more, and he was anxious to find them. For evidence, and for certainty that Scout and her child really were in the car that had driven away.

If not, they were somewhere else.

Somewhere closer.

He scanned the edge of the copse of trees that butted against the road. If he'd been scared for his life, he'd have run there, looked for a place to hide.

Protocol dictated that Boone back off, let the local P.D. do their job. It was what Chance would want him to do. It was what Boone probably would have done if he'd witnessed only the accident or even the kidnapping.

But Boone had spoken to Scout Cramer. He'd seen the fear in her eyes. He'd looked into her daughter's face and been reminded of what he'd lost. What he could only pray that he would one day get back.

He couldn't back off. Not yet.

A sound drifted through the quiet night. Soft. Like the mew of a kitten. Boone cocked his head to the side.

"Did you hear that?" he asked Lamar.

He knew the officer had. He'd stopped talking and was staring into the woods. "Could have been an animal," he said, but Boone doubted he believed it.

"Or a baby," Boone replied, heading for the trees.

"You think it's the missing child? How old did you say she was?"

"Two? Maybe three." *Cute as a button.* That was what

his mother would have said. Probably what his dad would have said. They loved kids. Would have loved to know their first granddaughter.

Boone would have loved to know his only child.

In God's time...

He'd heard the words so many times, from so many well-meaning people, that he almost never talked about his marriage, about his daughter, about anything that had to do with his life before HEART.

"It's possible she was thrown from the car. I didn't see a car seat."

"She was in one."

Lamar raised a dark brow and scowled. "I'm not going to ask why you know so much about this lady and her child. You're sure the kid was in the car seat?"

"Positive."

"If the car seat was installed wrong, it still could have been thrown from the car. Wouldn't have gone far, but a child that age could undo the harness and get out. She's young to be out on a night like tonight, but I'd rather her be out in the woods than in a car with a monster." Lamar sighed. "Wait here. I'll go take a look around."

Wasn't going to happen.

Boone followed him into the thick copse of trees, his gaze on the beam of light that illuminated the leaf-strewn ground.

"Anyone out here?" Officer Lamar called.

No response. Just the quiet rustle of leaves and the muted sound of distant sirens.

"We should split up," Boone suggested. "The more area we cover, the better."

"I'll call in our K-9 team. That will help. In the meantime, you need to go back to the car. There's a ravine a couple of hundred feet from here. You fall into that and—"

"I'm a former army ranger, Officer Lamar. I think I can handle dark woods and a deep ravine." He said it casually and walked away. They were wasting time arguing. Time he'd rather spend searching.

If the little girl *had* been thrown from the car on impact, the sooner they got her to the hospital, the better. But he didn't think she'd been thrown. He'd seen Scout buckle her in. She'd been secure. Someone had taken her from the station wagon. That same person could have tossed her into the trees, thrown her down the embankment, disposed of her like so much trash.

He'd seen it before, in places where no child should ever be. He'd carried nearly dead little girls from hovels that had become their prisons.

Rage filled him, clawing at his gut and threatening to steal every bit of reason he had. He didn't give in to it. He'd learned a lot from his father. Watching him deal with the foster kids his parents had taken in had taught Boone everything he needed to know about keeping cool, working with clear vision, not allowing his emotions to rule.

"Baby?!" he called, because he didn't know the child's name, and because a scared little girl might respond to a stranger's voice.

Then again, she might not.

She might stay silent, waiting and hoping for her mother's return.

Was that how it had been for Kendal? Had she been dropped off and left somewhere with strangers? Had she cried for her mother?

He shuddered.

That was another place he wouldn't allow his mind to go. Ever.

"Hello?" he tried again, and this time he heard a faint response. Not a child's cry. More like an adult's groan.

He headed toward the sound, picking his way through narrow saplings and thick pine trees, the shadowy world swaying with the soft November wind.

He heard another groan. This one so close, he knew he could reach out and touch the injured person. He scanned the ground, saw what looked like a pile of cloth and leaves under a heavy-limbed oak and sprinted to it.

Scout lay on her stomach, pale braid dark with blood, her face pressed into leaves and dirt. For a moment, he thought she was dead, and his heart jerked with the thought and with the feeling that he was too late to make a difference. Again.

Then his training kicked in, and he knelt, brushing back the braid, feeling for a pulse. She shifted, moaning softly, jerking up as if she thought she could jump up and run.

"Don't move," he muttered, the amount of blood seeping into her hair, splattering the leaves, seeping into the earth alarming. He needed Stella. All her years of working as a navy nurse made her a crucial and important part of HEART. It wasn't just that, though. She had a way of moving beyond emotion, filtering everything external and unnecessary and focusing on what needed to be done. He coveted that during their most difficult missions.

Scout either didn't hear his demand or didn't want to follow it. She twisted from his hand, the movement sluggish and slow, her face pale and streaked with so much blood, he thought they might lose her before an ambulance arrived.

He needed to find the source of the blood, but when he moved toward her, she jerked back, struggling to her knees and then her feet, swaying, her eyes wide and blank. "Lucy," she said clearly, that one word, that name enunciated.

"Was she with you?" he asked, easing closer, afraid to move quickly and scare her again.

"She's gone," she whispered. "He took her."

That was it. Just those words, and all the strength seemed to leave her body. She crumpled, and he just managed to catch her before she hit the ground.

Footsteps crashed behind him, sirens blaring loudly. An ambulance, but he was terrified that it was too late.

He ripped off his coat, pressed the sleeve to an oozing wound on her temple, the long furrowed gash so deep he could see bone. He knew a bullet wound when he saw one, knew exactly how close she'd come to dying.

His blood ran cold, every hair on the back of his neck standing on end. Someone had come very close to killing Scout, and that someone had Lucy.

"Is this the woman?" Officer Lamar panted up behind him, the beam of his flashlight splashing on leaves wet with blood.

He knelt beside Boone, touched Scout's neck. "We need to get that ambulance in here. Now!" he shouted into his radio.

Voices carried on the night air, footsteps pounding on leaves and packed earth. Branches breaking, time ticking and a little girl was being carried farther and farther away from her mother, and if something didn't change, a mother was being carried farther and farther away from her daughter.

He pressed harder, praying desperately that the flow of blood would be stanched before every bit of Scout's life slipped away.

THREE

Lucy!

Scout tried to call for her daughter, but the words stuck in her throat, fell into the darkness that seemed to be consuming her. She tried to struggle up from it, to push away the heavy veil that blocked her vision, but her arms were lead weights, her body refusing to move.

She tried again, and nothing but a moan emerged.

"I think she's waking up," a woman said, the voice unfamiliar, but somehow comforting. She wasn't alone in the darkness.

"I hope you're right. Until she does, we've got nothing to go on," a man responded, his soft drawl reminding her of something. Someone. She searched through the darkness, trying to find the memory, but there was nothing but the quiet beep of a machine and the soft rasp of cloth as someone moved close.

"Scout?" the man said.

Someone touched her cheek, and that one moment of contact was enough to pull her through the darkness. She opened her eyes, looked into a face she thought she knew. Dark red hair, blue eyes, hard jaw covered with fiery stubble.

"Who are you?" she asked, her voice thick, her throat hot.

Where am I?

Where is Lucy?

That last was the question she needed answered most. It was the *only* question that mattered.

She shoved aside blankets and sheets, tried to sit up.

"Not a good idea," the woman said, moving in beside the man and frowning. She had paler red hair. Cropped short in a pixie cut.

"I need to find my daughter," Scout managed to say, the words pounding through her head and echoing in her ears. Sharp pain shot through her temple, and she felt dizzy and sick, but she wouldn't lie down until she knew where Lucy was.

"We're looking for her," the man said, his expression grim and hard, his eyes a deep dark blue that Scout knew she had seen before.

"*I* need to look for her," she murmured, but her thoughts were scattering like dry leaves on a windy day, dancing along through the darkness that seemed to want to steal her away again.

"You're not in any shape to look for anyone," the woman said, dragging a chair across the floor and sitting. "We're going to do this for you, and you're going to have to trust that we can handle it."

The words were probably meant to comfort her, but they only filled Scout with panic. Lucy was missing. That was the only clear thought she had. Everything else was a blur of feeling and pain, bits of memories and shadowy images that she couldn't quite hold on to. A store. A man. Flames and smoke.

"I don't know who you are," she responded absently, her attention jumping from the woman to the man, then past them both. A hospital room with cream walls and an empty corkboard. A television mounted to a wall. A clock. In the background, Christmas music played, the carol as familiar as air.

"I'm Stella Silverstone. I work for HEART Incorporated." The woman took a card from her pocket and set it on a table near the bed. "Among other things, we help find the missing."

Missing. The word was like a dagger to the heart, and Scout had had enough. Enough listening. Enough talking. Enough sitting in a hospital room.

"I'm going to find my daughter." She scrambled from the bed, dizzy, sick, blankets puddling near her feet. "She's—"

"Been gone for three days," Stella said, the blunt words like hammers to the heart. "Running out of the hospital in some mad dash to find her isn't going to do any good."

"Stella," the man warned. "Let's take things slow."

"How slow do you want to take them, Boone? Because I'd say three days waiting to talk to the only witness is slow enough. I'm going to find Lamar. He's hanging around here somewhere."

She stalked from the room, closing the door firmly as she left. The sound reverberated through Scout's head, sent stars dancing in front of her eyes.

"You need to lie down." The man nudged her back to the bed, and she sat because she didn't think her legs could hold her.

"What happened?" she murmured to herself and to him, because she couldn't remember anything but those few images and the deep, deep fear for her daughter. It sat in her stomach, leaden and hard, the knot growing bigger with every passing moment.

"That's what we've been trying to find out." He sat in the chair his friend had abandoned, his elbows on his knees, his gaze direct.

"We've met before," she offered, the words ringing oddly in her ears.

"You remember." He smiled, but it didn't soften his expression. "I'm Boone Anderson."

The name was enough to bring a flood of memories— a trip to Walmart, Lucy in the cart. The man she'd been sure was following her. Boone handing her his business card.

And then...

What?

She pressed shaking fingers to her head, wanting to ease the deep throbbing pain. A thick bandage covered her temple, the edges folding as she ran her hand along them.

"Careful," Boone said, pulling her hand away and holding it lightly in his. "You're still stapled together."

"Tell me what happened," she responded, because she didn't care about the staples, the head injury, the IV line attached to her arm. All she cared about was getting up and going, but she didn't even know where to start, couldn't remember anything past the moment Boone had handed her his card. "Tell me where my daughter is," she added.

Please, God, let this be a nightmare. Please, let me wake up and see Lucy lying in her little toddler bed.

"We don't know much, Scout," he responded. "What we do know is that you were shopping. When you left the store, you were followed. The tire of your car was shot out, and you were in an accident."

She didn't care. Didn't want to know about the car or the accident or being followed. She needed to know about Lucy. "Just tell me what happened to my daughter."

"We don't know. You were alone when we found you."

"I need to go home." She jumped up, the room spinning. The knot in her stomach growing until it was all she could feel. "Maybe she's there."

She knew it was unreasonable, knew it couldn't be true, but she had to look, had to be sure.

"The police have already been to your house," he said gently. "She's not there."

"She could be hiding. She doesn't like strangers." Her voice trembled. Her body trembled, every fear she'd ever had, every nightmare, suddenly real and happening and completely outside of her control.

"Scout." He touched her shoulder, his fingers warm through thin cotton. She didn't want warmth, though. She wanted her child.

"Please," she begged. "I have to go home. I have to see for myself. I have to."

He eyed her for a moment, silent. Solemn. Something in his eyes that looked like the grief she was feeling, the horror she was living.

Finally, he nodded. "Okay. I'll take you."

Just like that. Simple and easy as if the request didn't go against logic. As if she weren't hooked to an IV, shaking from fear and sorrow and pain.

He grabbed a blanket from the foot of the bed and wrapped it around her shoulders, then texted someone. She didn't ask who—she was too busy trying to keep the darkness from taking her again. Too busy trying to remember the last moment she'd seen Lucy. Had she been scared? Crying?

Three days.

That was what Stella had said.

Three days that Lucy had been missing, and Scout had been lying in a hospital unaware. She closed her eyes, sick with the knowledge.

Please, God, let her be okay.

She was all Scout had. The only thing that really mattered to her. She had to be okay.

A tear slipped down her cheek. She didn't have the energy to wipe it away. Didn't have the strength to even open her eyes when Boone touched her cheek.

"It's going to be okay," he said quietly, and she wanted to believe him almost as much as she wanted to open her eyes and see her daughter.

"How can it be?"

"Because you ran into the right person the night your daughter was taken," he responded, and he sounded so confident, so certain of the outcome, she looked into his face, his eyes. Saw those things she'd seen before, but something else, too—faith, passion, belief.

"Who are you?"

"I already told you—Boone Anderson. I work for HEART. A hostage-rescue team based in Washington, D.C."

Someone knocked on the door, and Stella bustled in. Slim and athletic, she moved with a purposeful stride, her steps short and quick. "I'm not happy about this, Boone."

"I didn't think you would be," he responded, stepping aside.

"She's not ready to be released," she continued as she pulled on gloves and lifted Scout's arm. "You're not ready," she reiterated, looking straight into Scout's eyes. "You have a hairline fracture to your skull, staples in your forehead and a couple more days of recovery in the hospital before you should be going anywhere."

"I need to find—"

"Your daughter." Stella cut her off. "Yeah. I know. And she needs her mother's brain to be functioning well enough to help with our search." She pulled the IV from Scout's arm and pressed a cotton ball to the blood that bubbled up. "But I'm not going to waste time arguing with a parent's love. I've seen men and women do some crazy things for their kids."

She slapped a bandage over the cotton ball and straightened. "So, fine. We'll head over to your place. You can look around to your heart's content. Don't expect me to scrape you up off the ground, though. You fall, and I'm—"

"Stella…" Boone cut into her diatribe. Scout looked as if she was about to collapse, her face so pale he wasn't sure she'd make it into a wheelchair. "How about we just focus on the mission?"

"What mission?" she muttered. "This is pro bono, and I'm only helping because you saved my hide in Mexico City. If you remember correctly, I'm still supposed to be on medical leave."

"For the little scratch you got on the last mission? I'd have been back to work the next day," he scoffed, because he knew she wanted him to, knew that asking her if she was up to going back to work would only irritate her.

"If I remember correctly," she responded, her eyes

flashing, "you took two weeks off for that little concussion you got in Vietnam."

It had been a fractured skull, and he'd been forced to take a month off, but he didn't correct her. "True, but I'm not as pain tolerant as you are. I need a little more time to recover from my injuries."

She snorted. "We have some clothes around here for the lady? I don't think she wants to leave in a hospital gown."

"Just what she was admitted in." He pointed to a pile of belongings. He'd been through the purse, the pockets of the coat and jeans. He'd found nothing that might point him to a kidnapper.

"I'll help her get dressed. You wait in the hall."

"I don't need help," Scout murmured. "If you just call a cab for me, I'll get dressed and—"

"Not going to happen, sweetie," Stella said. "You go with us or you don't go at all."

"Says who?"

"Says the people who are looking for your daughter for free," Stella bit out.

"What Stella means," Boone cut in, "is that you're weak and you need to be careful."

"What I mean is that if we're going to do this, I want to get it done. Besides, if we don't go now, Lamar might show up and put a stop to our little party."

"We're not sneaking her out of here, Stella. It isn't that kind of mission."

"Whatever kind it is, Lamar isn't going to be happy that you're taking his only witness. He's been waiting three days to question her, and if he weren't following a lead that was called in—"

"What lead?" Scout asked, her eyes alive with hope.

He'd seen it many times before, watched hope flare and then die only to flare again. He knew the feeling, knew the quick grip of the heart when it seemed as if what was longed for would finally be had. Knew the despair when it wasn't.

"Don't know," Stella responded. If she noticed Scout's sudden excitement, she didn't let on. She wasn't one to give false hope, and she wasn't one to feed dreams. "I just know he left. Said he wouldn't be gone long. So, how about we get this show on the road?" She looked at Boone, pointed at the door. "Out."

He went because she was right. If they were going, now was the time. Lamar wouldn't be happy that they'd helped his lone witness walk out of the hospital. On the other hand, he had no reason to keep her there.

Except to protect her.

She'd nearly died and had lost so much blood, she'd been given five units her first night in the hospital. Whoever had taken her child hadn't planned on Scout surviving.

Why?

Who?

They were questions the police were desperately trying to answer with little to no success. They'd reviewed security footage from the store and parking lot, tried to ID the man who'd been following Scout. He'd been careful, though, his face always turned away from the cameras as if he'd known exactly where they were. No license plates had been visible on the cars that had followed her. No clear image of any of the drivers. The kidnapping had been planned by someone who knew exactly what he was doing. Lamar and his team weren't denying it, and they were doing everything in their power to find the people responsible.

The problem was, there were no good leads. No one who'd really seen anything. Most people had been caught up in preholiday daze and hadn't noticed Scout or Lucy. If they'd noticed her, they hadn't noticed the man who'd followed them around the store.

Three days on the phone with Chance, convincing him that using HEART resources was the only way to bring Lucy home, and Boone was just tired enough to feel as though he was biting off more than he could chew. He couldn't let the case go, though. He wouldn't, because he didn't want another parent to go through what he had. He didn't want anyone to ever have to spend every second, minute, hour of every day wondering where their loved one was.

Yeah. He was going to search for Lucy, and he was going to do everything in his power to bring her home safely. God willing, that would happen.

In the meantime, he'd promised Chance that he'd keep his nose clean, that he wouldn't overstep the boundaries or smash any local P.D. toes while he was working on the case.

He wasn't sure taking their sole witness from the hospital was the way to do it, but he'd seen the look in Scout's eyes before. Seen it in the gaze of every mother, father, uncle, aunt, brother, sister, loved one who'd lost someone. She'd do what she thought she had to in order to bring her daughter home. If that meant sneaking out of the hospital alone, she'd do it.

And sneaking out alone when someone had nearly killed her?

That wasn't such a great idea.

He pulled out his cell phone and dialed Lamar's number. The call went straight to voice mail. He left a message, figuring that was as good as asking permission.

Chance wouldn't see it that way, but Boone figured he was following the letter of the law. For now, that would have to be good enough.

FOUR

Please let me wake up from this nightmare.

The prayer flitted through Scout's throbbing head as Stella pushed her wheelchair outside. The full moon glowed from a pitch-black sky, the frigid November air slicing through her T-shirt and coat. Someone had washed all of her clothes, but she still thought she could smell the coppery scent of blood. Somewhere people were having a conversation, their voices drifting through the quiet night. A nightmare wouldn't be so full of details. A nightmare wouldn't let her feel the first drop of icy rain on her cheek or smell the frosty dampness of the air.

Lucy.

Gone.

The thought lodged in her head and stayed there. The only real thought she could hold on to.

An SUV pulled up to the curb and Stella opened the door, took Scout's arm and helped her in. "Seat belt," she barked, and Scout fumbled to snap it into place.

Her hands trembled, but somehow she managed. She wanted one thing. To find her daughter. Everything else—

the throbbing pain in her head, the sick feeling in her stomach, the fear that made her chest ache—didn't matter.

Boone didn't ask for an address or directions to her house. He just pulled away from the hospital, merging into light traffic on the main road that led through River Valley.

Scout knew exactly what she'd see on her way home. Dark trees stretching toward the moonlit sky, houses dotting the landscape, a few cars meandering along. She watched the landscape flying by, her eyes heavy with fatigue. She felt weaker than she wanted to, and she couldn't afford to be weak. Not with Lucy missing.

Boone turned into her neighborhood, bypassing the bigger fancier houses and weaving his way through main roads and side streets. He was familiar with the neighborhood and must have been to her house on several occasions. It wasn't easy to find, tucked away from the road, the driveway long and winding. In the next lot over, Mrs. Geoffrey's house was dark, the porch light off. She'd been planning to visit family for Thanksgiving and had asked Scout and Lucy to come along.

They should have gone.

Boone turned into the driveway, slowing as overgrown trees brushed the sides of the SUV. In the spring, Scout would have them trimmed. Her rent-to-own lease allowed her the luxury of doing whatever she wanted to the tiny little rancher and the acre it sat on.

The lights were off at the house. She hadn't left them that way. She always left the porch light burning and the foyer light on. Too many dark shadows around the house at night, and even with Mrs. Geoffrey just a few hundred yards away, Scout always worried that someone might be waiting in the gloomy recesses of the yard.

Tonight, she had nothing to fear. She'd already lost everything. There was nothing more that could be done to hurt her. She opened the door as the car coasted to a stop, might have jumped out and run to the house if Stella hadn't grabbed her arm.

"Slow down, sister! You want to kill yourself before we find your kid?"

She didn't respond. The car had come to a full stop, and she wasn't waiting any longer. She stumbled out, nearly falling to her knees, her body refusing to cooperate with her brain's commands.

Just move! she thought. *It's easy.*

Only it wasn't. Her legs wobbled as she took a step toward the house, her purse thumping against her side. The keys were in it, and she needed to pull them out, but she wasn't sure how she was going to manage that and the walk.

"How about you not go rushing out of the SUV like that again?" Boone stepped into place beside her, his arm sliding around her waist. In another lifetime, she would have blushed at the zip of electricity that seemed to shoot through her at his touch. In this lifetime, she just wanted to get into the house, go into Lucy's room, make sure that her daughter wasn't waiting there for her.

"If I were rushing, I'd already be in the front door," she responded through gritted teeth.

"If you were *thinking,* you'd have realized that anyone could be waiting out here. It's a nice dark area. No streetlights. No neighbors around. You're an easy target. Might as well put a bull's-eye on your chest and stand out in the middle of Main Street," he drawled.

She hadn't been thinking about that.

Now she was, and she couldn't shake the feeling

that someone was watching. She shivered, fishing in her purse for keys that weren't there.

She dug deeper, found her wallet, cell phone, spare change. The little rag doll that Lucy loved. She pulled it out, her heart burning with tears that she wouldn't shed. Crying couldn't bring her daughter back.

"My keys," she began, but Boone had keys in his hand. Her keys—heart key chain with three keys: one for the front door, one for the back, one for the car.

"The police used them to access your place when they were looking for Lucy. They returned them last night."

And he'd taken them.

She didn't know how she felt about that, didn't think it really mattered.

The police *had* searched her house, just as Boone had said.

Lucy wasn't in there.

She felt defeated, sick to her stomach and ready to collapse, but she was going to look in the house anyway, because she didn't know what else to do.

The door swung open on creaky hinges. She'd been meaning to oil them, but time had got away from her— all the busyness of going to work and being a mother had made anything extra nearly impossible to do.

She walked into the dark living room, inhaling stale air and silence. No sound of Lucy giggling. No soft pad of little-girl feet on the floor. No squeals or cries. Nothing. The house felt empty and lonely and horrible.

Her foot caught on something, and she fell forward, would have hit the ground if Boone hadn't grabbed her arm.

"Careful," he said.

"There's something on the floor. I think it's the couch cushion."

"How about we turn on a light. Then you'll know for sure," Stella said drily.

The light went on, illuminating a room that had been taken apart. Couch cushions slashed and tossed on the floor, books torn and flung away. Photographs ripped from walls, their frames smashed. Lucy's little stuffed bear near the fireplace, its stuffing hanging out like entrails.

She started toward it, but Boone grabbed her arm. "Not yet."

"What—?"

"Take her outside." Boone cut her off, his face hard, his expression unreadable.

That was it. A quick sharp command, and Stella grabbed Scout's arm, started dragging her back toward the door.

Only she wasn't going, because this was her house, her daughter, her problem to solve. No matter how sick she felt, no matter how scared she was.

She yanked away. "I need to check Lucy's room," she mumbled, more to herself than to either of the people who'd brought her home.

"Not going to happen, sister." Stella tightened her grip, dragging Scout backward with enough force to nearly throw her off balance. She had a choice. Go or fight. Normally, she'd go, because she was a rule follower, the kind of person who'd never take a stroller on an escalator or park in a no-parking zone. She didn't try the grapes at the grocery store before she paid for them or take fifteen items into the twelve-items-or-less line.

But she had to find Lucy. Had to.

And if that meant fighting, that was what she was going to do.

She yanked her arm from Stella's, tried to run through the living room and into the hallway beyond. It should have been easy. She jogged nearly every day, sprinted after Lucy all the time, across the backyard, through the local park.

But her legs didn't want to move, and she stumbled forward, moving in what seemed like slow motion, the hallway so far away she wasn't sure she'd ever get to it.

"Not a good choice, Scout," Boone sighed.

Next thing she knew, she was in his arms, heading back the few feet she'd managed to go. Outside again, the cold November air stung her cheeks, and she wasn't even sure how she'd got there, where she was going, what she was looking for.

Lucy.

She zeroed in on the thought and held on to it, because she couldn't seem to hold on to anything else.

"Put me down!" She wiggled in his arms, trying to free herself. He just held on more tightly, striding to the SUV and opening the door. He set her in the backseat, leaned down so they were eye to eye.

"Do us both a favor," he growled, "and stay there."

He closed the door and walked away. She would have opened it and followed, but Stella was right there, hips against the door, back to Scout.

Scout slid across the bucket seat, reached for the handle on the other side, heard a soft click and a beep. She tried the handle. The door wouldn't open. She climbed over the seat and into the front, pushed the button to unlock the doors. Nothing.

Someone tapped on the window, and she looked out,

met Stella's eyes. "Not going to open, sister," Stella called through the glass. "We've got a special lock system for situations like this."

Like what? Scout wanted to ask, but Stella turned away, her attention focused on the edge of the property and the oversize trees that lined it.

Standing guard?

That was what it seemed as though she was doing—putting herself and her life on the line for Scout.

Why?

It was another question Scout wanted to ask.

Later.

First, she needed to find a way out of the SUV and back in the house. Lucy might not be there. *Wasn't there.* She admitted it to herself, because living in a fantasy world wouldn't help her get Lucy back. She had to be practical, had to be smart, had to trust that her daughter was okay and that they'd be reunited eventually.

If she didn't, she'd fall apart. That wouldn't do anyone any good.

She pressed a shaky finger to her temple, the bandage scratchy and thick, the throbbing pain of the wound it covered making her stomach churn.

"Concentrate," she muttered, looking around for some other method of opening the doors.

Maybe the hatchback?

Hadn't she seen something in a survival show about unlatching trunks from the inside? Was it possible to do the same with the hatchback opening of an SUV?

She crawled back over the seat, her stomach heaving as pain shot through her temple. Cold sweat beaded her brow, and her entire body seemed to be shaking, but she managed to get to the back section of the vehicle. She felt around for a mechanism that would open the door, found nothing.

Two police cars pulled into the driveway, lights flashing, sirens off. Scout stayed where she was as several police officers ran past. She didn't think they saw her lying on her side in the back of Boone's SUV. She doubted it would matter if they did. They weren't going to let her out of the vehicle, and Stella hadn't budged from her place near the passenger door.

Lights splashed out from the windows of the little rancher she'd lived in for three years. She knew each window, each light. Named them silently as they flashed on. Dining room at the side of the house. Her room in the front. Lucy's room. Behind the house, trees butted up against the night sky, the canopy of the forest illuminated by moonlight. She knew exactly how far the kitchen light would spill out from the window above the sink, knew just how much of the backyard would be painted gold by it.

Her heart thudded painfully as shadows moved in front of the window. Somewhere, her daughter was sleeping in a strange bed, in a strange house, with strangers all around.

Best-case scenario, she was.

Worst-case scenario…

Scout refused to put a name to it, refused to allow herself to imagine anything other than her daughter lying in bed crying for her.

She closed her eyes, trying to pray, wanting to pray. Her mind was empty of anything but fear and sorrow and the aching pain of her injury.

A car engine broke the silence of the night, and she managed to crawl back over the seat. She sat there as a small Toyota pulled up behind the police cars. Scout knew the car. It belonged to her landlady, Eleanor Finch. The police must have called to let her know there'd been a break-in at the property.

Eleanor got out of the car, but she didn't approach the house, just stood and stared at it. Maybe this was old hat for her. She owned a number of properties in River Valley. Most of them were a lot more impressive and lucrative than this one. Scout figured that was why she'd been willing to do a rent-to-own contract on the rancher. It didn't rent for enough to make it worth Eleanor's while to keep it.

She hadn't ever asked, though. Eleanor liked her privacy. She wasn't warm and fuzzy. Nor was she approachable. She'd insisted on three months' rent as a deposit and the contract read that she got to keep it if Scout decided to break her lease.

That had been fine with Scout. She hadn't intended to break the three-year lease, because she'd pictured living there forever with Lucy. A nice little place in a nice little town filled with lots of nice people. Good schools. Pretty little church. Everything clean and tidy.

Only it wasn't anymore, and maybe the house wasn't going to be a place for forever. Maybe it was just a stopgap on the way to somewhere else.

Eleanor pulled out her cell phone and made a call, her gaze still on the house. Scout wanted to get out of the SUV and talk to her, but the doors were still locked tight and Stella was still standing guard. There was nothing Scout could do but wait and wonder what was going on in the house and when someone was going to come out and tell her about it.

* * *

Boone had been hoping for a ransom note. There hadn't been one. No prints on the furniture, doors, pieces of broken frame. He watched as the local police processed the scene, staying out of their way because he didn't want to get kicked out. He needed information. The more the better. Unfortunately, there wasn't much to be had. Someone had torn the house apart.

Maybe more than someone.

Maybe several people.

Going through a house as thoroughly as this one had been gone through would have taken one person a few hours. A couple of people working together could have accomplished the job much more quickly.

He walked down the hall, bypassing a uniformed officer who was dusting the bathroom door for prints. Even that room had been torn apart, medicine cabinet emptied, a picture pulled off the wall and taken apart, the frame in pieces on the floor.

Lamar was two doors down, taking pictures of Lucy's room. Like the others, it was a wreck, the mattress on the toddler bed slashed, the stuffing strewn all over the floor. Stuffed animals had been dismembered, picture books thrown from shelves. It looked as if a hurricane had blown through.

"Find anything interesting?" he asked, and Lamar frowned.

"I should make you leave. This is a crime scene."

"I've been in more than a few of them. I'll be careful not to contaminate anything. Did you find anything?"

"Aside from a mess? No. Whoever did this was careful. No prints on the doorknobs or any other surface in the house. I pulled a couple of kid prints off the underside of the bed in here, but nothing else."

"Someone wiped things down?"

"Thoroughly." Lamar nearly spat the word out, the look on his face a mixture of disgust and frustration.

"Awfully knowledgeable petty thieves," Boone said, even though he didn't think the ransacking had anything to do with thievery. It had everything to do with the fact that Lucy was missing. He was sure of that; he just wasn't sure what the connection was.

"Neither of us believes that thieves did this," Lamar muttered.

"You have any leads on the kidnappers?"

"Nothing. I'm hoping I can get a description from Scout tonight. If she got a good look at our perp, we may finally have a lead." He eyed Boone for a moment. "Speaking of Scout, I don't suppose you want to explain why you brought her here."

"She wanted to come."

"Sometimes my son wants to come to work with me, but he's six, so I have to tell him it's not a good idea."

"Scout isn't six. She's a grown woman, and she was going to find a way here with or without my help. I figured it was better to give her my help and a little protection."

"Maybe next time, you can convince her to wait for the police instead."

"I'm hoping there won't be a next time."

"I wouldn't count on that, Anderson. Things aren't making sense, and in my experience that means there's a lot going on under the surface, a lot we don't know about, a lot that could cause Scout serious trouble."

"She's already *in* serious trouble." Boone pointed out the obvious, and Lamar frowned.

"Not your problem. I've been allowing your team to do some investigating, but that stops if you get in my way."

"Maybe you should explain what that entails so I can avoid it."

"Let's try this on for size," Lamar responded. "You don't take a witness out of the hospital without permission from me. You don't take her to undisclosed locations or hide her away somewhere for safekeeping, either."

"Seeing as how she's sitting in my SUV waiting for us to finish in here, I'd say she's not exactly hiding."

"I'm making it clear for future reference, because if she suddenly disappears, your entire team is going to be on the line for it."

"What's that supposed to mean?" It took a lot to get him riled up, but Boone was heading there. He stayed out of the way. He played nice. He'd followed Chance's rules of engagement with local police. What he wasn't going to do was stand there and take it while HEART was used as a scapegoat.

"It hasn't escaped my notice that you were the last person aside from Scout to see Lucy—"

"Don't go there, Lamar." He bit the words out. "Because if you do, I'll go here—you and your team need as much help as you can get on this. Turning away an organization that has made its name freeing hostages and bringing them home safely isn't the smart way to go."

"I know who you work for, and I know what HEART does. What I don't know is why you're wasting time on this case when there are bigger, more lucrative cases you could be tackling."

"Because it isn't about money. It's about family," he retorted, full-out riled, and he'd better not let it show. He'd made that mistake on one too many occasions, and local police hadn't much appreciated it. Neither had Chance. Boone didn't care all that much, but if he wanted to help Scout, he needed to play things smart.

"Everything is about money, Anderson. You work this job enough, and you start to realize it," Lamar said wearily as he used gloved hands to lift a photo from the floor. Nearly ripped in two, it was a close-up of Scout and Lucy taken when Lucy was a baby. Probably one of those Sears or Walmart portraits. It shouldn't have been beautiful. The background was a little too bright, the lighting a little harsh, but Scout looked soft and sweet, her expression so filled with love it made Boone's heart ache. He'd seen that look in Lana's eyes the day Kendal was born.

Had it been there after that?

He didn't remember. He'd been out of town a lot, working missions that he couldn't talk about in places he wasn't allowed to reveal. He'd missed out on weeks and months of memories. Some days that hurt worse than others. Today, looking at the photo of Scout smiling at a sleeping Lucy, it hurt a lot.

"I'll wait outside," he said abruptly, because he didn't want to stand in the doorway of the nursery any longer, thinking about his daughter, who was out in the world somewhere. Lost to him until he could find her again.

FIVE

Scout wanted to sleep.

She wanted it so badly she was trying to force herself into it. No amount of trying to slip away from reality worked, though. No matter how much she tried, she was still in the SUV watching police officers enter and exit her house.

She glanced at Eleanor. She was still standing near her car, but she wasn't alone. A police officer was beside her, jotting something in a notebook as she spoke.

Stella hadn't moved from her position. As a matter of fact, Scout wasn't sure she'd blinked in the time since they'd left the house.

She knocked on the window, and Stella glanced her way, then turned toward the yard again.

She knocked again.

Nothing. Not even a flinch or twitch.

"I know you can hear me," she yelled.

"I am ignoring you," Stella yelled back.

"You're going to have to acknowledge me eventually." She hoped.

Again. Nothing.

She settled back into the seat, closed her eyes, heard the quiet click of the locks.

Free?

She tried the door. It opened.

"Don't get out," Stella commanded without looking her way.

"I have to," she responded, opening the door wider, ready to hop out and go inside.

"You want your little girl to have to raise herself?" There was no emotion in Stella's voice. Nothing to indicate that she cared one way or another.

"My little girl is missing. Until I find her, that question is moot." She levered out of the car, swaying as the blood rushed from her head.

"Told you not to get out," Stella grumbled, grabbing her arm and holding her up when she might have fallen over. "You're still weak. The way I see it, you should be in the hospital. Since I'm not running the show, I guess you're going to be wherever Boone decides we're going to take you."

Wherever Boone decided?

She didn't think so, but he was walking toward them, his long legs eating up the ground between them, his dark red hair slightly ruffled as if he'd run his fingers through it a few dozen times.

"Did they find anything?" Scout asked. *Did they find her?*

She didn't ask the second question. She knew the answer.

"The place was wiped clean." He glanced at Stella and some secret message seemed to pass between them. She didn't like it. She didn't want to be left on the outside looking in.

"Professionals?" Stella's arms were folded across her

chest, her stance wide. She looked larger-than-life but was probably only an inch taller than Scout.

"Looks that way."

"Guess we have a lot of questions that are going to need answering. Does Lamar want us to keep her here or take her back to the hospital to wait?"

"I'm right here, and I don't care what Lamar wants," Scout cut in. She sounded weaker than she wanted to, her voice faint.

"I was thinking the same." Boone smiled, his eyes crinkling at the corners. He looked a few years older than she was. Maybe in his early to mid-thirties, his body lean and muscular. The kind of guy who'd get attention wherever he went because of his good looks and his deep red hair. "Unfortunately, my boss does care, and he'll be mighty unhappy if we drive away without Officer Lamar's permission."

"Mighty?" Stella sighed. "Who says that?"

"Me and everyone I grew up with." He took Scout's arm. "How about we go inside and see if there's anything missing?"

"If the rest of the house is as torn apart as the living room, I'm not sure I'll be able to tell," she admitted. She was half hoping that he'd say it wasn't, half believing that it couldn't possibly be.

"It's pretty well messed up, but you'll know if there's any jewelry or valuables missing."

"I don't have much." A few pieces of jewelry of her mother's. Her parents' wedding rings. Some china that had belonged to her great-grandmother and that had been passed down to Scout. Her parents hadn't been wealthy, and they hadn't believed in collecting frivolities.

"That will make things even easier." He urged her inside, closing the door firmly behind them. Stella hadn't followed them. Was she still standing guard outside?

Did they really think it was necessary?

There were police cars and police officers and neighbors who'd gathered near at the edge of the driveway. It would take someone with a lot of guts to try anything with so many witnesses.

Then again, it had taken someone with a lot of guts to follow her through a grocery store, run her off the road and take her daughter.

Several police officers stood in the living room. They were silent as she followed Boone through into the hallway.

They knew who she was, knew she was the mother of the missing child. Knew how heavy her heart must be. She wanted to tell them that no matter what they were imagining, it couldn't compare to what she actually felt. There were no words to describe the thousand-ton weight pressing on her chest, no vocabulary that existed that could express the depth of her fear.

"Where do you keep your valuables?" Boone asked.

"In my room."

"Then how about we look there first?"

She didn't tell him where it was, but he didn't slow his pace or ask. Lucy's room was to the right. Hers was across the hall. There was a spare room, too. She'd put a futon and a small dresser in it to fill the space. Not because she had family or friends who might come for a visit. She had no family left and she'd cut ties with her friends in San Jose after she'd become pregnant with Lucy. Only Amber knew where she'd gone after she'd moved, and she'd been as anxious to keep that secret as Scout had been.

Had she taken the secret to the grave with her?

Scout had assumed that she had. They were best friends, more like sisters than anything else. She couldn't imagine that Amber would have betrayed her trust. Especially when she was the one who'd been so determined that Scout leave San Jose, so determined that she not tell anyone ever who Lucy's father was.

She followed Boone into her bedroom, her stomach sick with dread. The mattress had been slashed, the stuffing pulled out. The same for her pillow and the down comforter she'd spent a small fortune on. Every picture on her dresser had been tossed on the floor. All her clothes were emptied into a pile. The small jewelry box lay broken a few feet from the bed as if someone had tossed it there. She crouched beside it, head spinning from moving too quickly.

The rings and jewelry were there. Under the broken wood and the tiny ballerina that used to spin each time the box opened. Her mother had received the box for her tenth birthday, and Scout had inherited it after her death. She'd treasured it for nearly fifteen years. Now it was gone.

She grabbed the rings, her eyes burning and her chest tight.

"They didn't take them," she said, meeting Boone's dark blue eyes.

"Didn't take what?" A tall dark-haired man walked into the room before Boone responded. Dressed in a police uniform, his shoes shined, his gaze sharp, the officer glanced at the jewelry box, then met Scout's eyes. "Your jewelry?"

"Yes."

"Does it have any value?"

"I don't know. I never had it appraised."

He frowned, lifting one of the thin gold chains. "Looks like real gold. I'd say whoever was in your house wasn't looking for valuables. They didn't take the television. Didn't take your laptop. Is there anything else they might have been looking for?"

"Like what?"

"Don't know, but I'm figuring you might."

"I don't." He was trying to get somewhere with his questioning, but her sluggish brain wasn't following.

"Most kids aren't abducted by strangers. You know that, right?"

"I—"

"That being the case," he continued, not giving her a chance to speak, "it seems reasonable to assume that the person who took your daughter wasn't a stranger."

She didn't say anything, because she was afraid he was right. She was afraid that the secret she'd kept had been revealed and the people she'd feared had come for her daughter.

"Maybe you know the person? Maybe you've had some kind of interaction with him? Are you dating someone? Were you in a relationship in the last couple of months?"

"No." She shook her head, regretted it immediately. She felt light-headed and unsteady. She tried to stand, to put herself closer to eye level with the officer rather than having him tower over her.

Her muscles didn't want to cooperate.

Boone took her hand, tugging up in one easy motion. "You okay?" he asked.

"Should I be?" she responded.

"No," he admitted, glancing around the room.

The officer's attention was on Scout, and it never wavered. He didn't look as if he believed her story. "How about someone you work with? Someone in your circle of friends?" he pressed.

"I work at the library," she said, her mouth cottony and dry. "When I'm not working, I'm here with Lucy. I go to church on Sunday, but other than that, my life is pretty boring."

"Yet someone kidnapped your daughter and ransacked your house. There has to be a reason for that."

"I guess so." She rubbed her forehead, her fingers flitting over the bandage. It did nothing to clear her thoughts. She thought she knew where he was going with the questions. Thought he was implying that she'd brought all this on herself.

Maybe she had.

She'd made mistakes. Little ones. Big ones.

She'd thought that she'd moved beyond them, made a life that wouldn't be touched by what she'd done, the lies she'd told.

She should have known better.

There were always consequences. Maybe not right away, but eventually.

"Guessing isn't going to help us find your daughter," the officer said. There wasn't any kindness in his tone or in his eyes. Maybe he was assuming that she'd had some part in Lucy's kidnapping. Maybe he thought she'd brought it on herself. "How about you tell me what you have that someone is searching for? Money? Drugs?"

"What? No!" she protested, because there wasn't anything that anyone might want in the house. "I'm not into that kind of thing."

"Then what are you into? People don't get into this

kind of trouble over nothing. Did you have a deal with someone? Did you get in over your head and not know where to turn for help?"

"I'm not the kind of person who gets into trouble, and I've never been into anything so much that I was over my head."

"This—" Lamar gestured to the slashed mattress, the picture frames smashed, the pile of clothes "—would prove otherwise. So, how about you be honest? Tell me what's going on?"

"How about you back off a little, Lamar?" Boone cut in, reaching down to grab the broken jewelry box from the floor and setting it on the dresser. He moved calmly, easily, no sign of tension. "She's still recovering from a serious injury."

"And her daughter is missing. Which is a more pressing matter?"

"Lucy is the most pressing," Scout cut in. She didn't want any time wasted. Not arguing or asking questions she had no answers to. "But I really don't have a boyfriend or an ex. I don't have a drug habit. I don't do anything illegal."

"Right." The officer pulled a business card from his wallet and handed it to her.

She glanced at it, read the name. Jet Lamar.

"Keep that with you," he continued. "If you remember anything, give me a call."

"There's nothing to remem—"

"And you!" He jabbed a finger at Boone. "Get her out of my crime scene and back to the hospital."

"Out of her house, you mean?" Boone responded.

"I want her out of here, and since you're the one who

made her escape from the hospital happen, I figure you should be the one to make that happen, too."

He stalked out of the room.

Scout would have followed, but her ears were buzzing, the light dimming.

"You don't look so hot." Boone wrapped an arm around her waist. A good thing, because her legs were weak, her heart beating a strange uneven rhythm.

"Just what every woman wants to hear," she murmured, the words slipping away before they really formed.

He must have heard, because he smiled and shook his head. "It's good that you have a sense of humor, Scout. That's going to help a lot."

Help what? This time the words didn't come out at all. They got stuck in her throat and stayed there as blackness edged in and her vision went fuzzy.

Someone said her name, but she wasn't sure if it was Boone or someone else. Her knees buckled, and Boone scooped her into his arms, muttering something that she didn't hear or couldn't comprehend. She wanted to close her eyes and give in and just let herself slip away. It was what she'd wanted desperately while she was waiting in the SUV. Now she fought it because she didn't want to go back to the hospital.

"Put me down." She shoved at a chest that was sculpted and hard and had absolutely no give in it.

"So you can fall on the floor? I don't think so." Boone stepped outside, the cold air filling her lungs and clearing her head. "I think it's time to get you out of here."

"I'm okay now. I want to stay."

"Sorry, but Lamar doesn't want you here. I'm trying to stay on his good side." He set her in the backseat of the SUV, leaning in to grab the end of her seat belt. They were eye to eye, his scent filling the vehicle, a mixture of soap and spicy aftershave.

"I don't want to go back to the hospital."

"So, we won't go there." He closed the door, slid into the driver's seat while Stella climbed into the passenger seat beside him.

"Let me guess," she said. "We're going to Raina's."

"She has plenty of room." He backed up, maneuvering the SUV around parked police cars and Eleanor's car.

"So does a hotel."

"Not as easy to secure."

"Jackson isn't going to like it."

"Sure he is. Right now, he's staying in a hotel. I think he'll be happy to have an excuse to spend more time at his fiancée's house before he returns to D.C."

Scout had no idea what they were talking about. She didn't ask. She was too busy going over what Officer Lamar had said. He seemed to think she had something that someone wanted.

The only thing she'd had that anyone might want was Lucy, and the only people who might be interested in having her didn't even know she existed.

Did they?

Don't ever tell them, Scout. Swear to me that you won't. They'll take that baby from you and you'll never see it again. You try to fight them, and it'll get ugly. They'll find some reason to throw you in jail or make CPS think you're not going to be a good mother. They might even do worse. I wouldn't put anything past my family.

Scout could still hear the words, still see Amber's face as she said them—pale and gaunt, her eyes hollow. Nearly four years later, the conversation still haunted her.

Amber had said that if her family knew Scout was pregnant with her half brother Christopher's child, they'd do everything in their power to gain custody.

That had scared Scout enough to send her running. The Schoepflins had power and lots of it. They came from a long line of politicians and socialites. According to Amber, the money came from a great-great-grandfather who'd made it big during the California gold rush. Maybe it was true. Maybe it wasn't. Amber had had a vivid imagination and a way of twisting the truth to fit her mood. Whatever the case, the Schoepflins had money, political clout and plenty of friends in high places.

Scout had herself.

And right then, sitting in the SUV with two other people, she felt more alone than she'd ever been in her life.

SIX

Boone glanced in the review mirror as he drove down the dirt road that led to Raina Lowery's place. They hadn't been followed. He'd taken a few unnecessary turns and woven his way through a few quiet neighborhoods just to be sure.

Jackson had made it to the house ahead of them, and he wasn't happy. He'd made that known—loudly—during a phone conversation with Stella.

One night.

That was what he'd finally promised after Boone had grabbed the phone and called in about three dozen favors he'd done for Jackson over the years.

One night would work if Lamar cleared Scout's house as a crime scene and let her return the following day. Boone was hoping that would be the case. If not, he'd have to make other arrangements. He could bring Scout to his D.C. apartment, but he didn't think she'd like that idea.

He pulled into Raina's driveway and parked behind Jackson's car. Almost every light in the house was on, the porch light glowing invitingly. He'd had a porch at the house he and Lana had shared. A porch swing, too.

He tried not to think about those things, but when he got tired, the memories were always at the surface, tempting him to spend some time exploring them.

Not tonight. He had to get Scout in the house, get her settled. Then he was going to call Lamar. He'd hinted that Scout might be involved in something illegal, that maybe she'd got herself in too deep. Boone wanted to know if Lamar had found evidence to support that or if he was just making a conjecture. He suspected the latter. He'd done his own research. Scout had been in River Valley for three years. She'd been working as a librarian in San Jose before that. No criminal record. Not even a traffic ticket. Her neighbor said she was quiet and sweet. Her coworkers sang her praises. If she was involved in anything illegal, there wasn't a person around who suspected it.

He opened her door, offering a hand as she slid out. She took it, her palm dry and cool. She had thin fingers and delicate bones, her steps shuffling and slow as he helped her to Raina's door. It opened before they reached it, Jackson hovering on the threshold. He didn't look happy.

"Took you guys a while," he commented as he stepped aside and allowed them to enter. "I thought you'd be here half an hour ago."

"Boone insisted on taking fifty side trips," Stella growled. She didn't look any happier than Jackson. Perfect. The two of them together should be fun.

"I wanted to make sure we weren't being followed. I didn't want any trouble following us here."

"Maybe you should have thought about that before you decided to use Raina's place as a safe house. We've got property in D.C. if you need it." Jackson glanced at Scout, his expression easing. Boone had known it would. One thing about Jackson: he always rooted for the underdog, always wanted to help the helpless. Right at that moment, Scout looked about as helpless as anyone could be, her skin pale, the bandage on her forehead sliding down over her eyebrow. "You must be Scout," he said. "I'm Jackson Miller. I was sorry to hear about your daughter's kidnapping."

"Me, too," she said quietly.

"My fiancée has a room ready for you. If you want to follow me—"

"Samuel and I can bring her there." Raina Lowery stepped into the foyer, her blond hair pulled back with a headband. She'd been through a lot the past few years, first losing her husband and son in a car accident, then being kidnapped while on a mission trip to Africa. Boone had been on the mission to rescue her and had helped out when she'd faced more trouble after her return to the States. He liked and respected her. He also liked her cooking.

And she had been cooking. He could smell it in the air, something spicy and probably delicious. Hopefully, there were leftovers.

Samuel stood beside her, his face just a little less gaunt than it had been a few months ago, his prosthesis barely noticeable beneath the sweatpants he wore.

"Hey, Sammy," Boone said and was rewarded with a shy smile.

"Hello, Daniel Boone! You shoot any bears today?" The kid had been reading every book about Daniel Boone that he could get his hands on and loved to joke with Boone about his name. After everything he'd been through, it was good to see him loosening up and having fun. He'd been a child soldier in Sudan, but had risked his life to save Raina. Things had been easier for him since Raina had brought him to the U.S. Hopefully, bringing someone who was obviously injured and in trouble into his home wouldn't send the kid back into fear and anxiety.

Boone frowned. He should have thought about that before he'd talked Jackson into letting Scout stay there.

Raina stepped forward and took Scout's arm. "Come with me. I'll get you tucked into bed and then bring you a nice cup of tea."

"I don't want you to go to any bother." Scout met Boone's eyes, silently begging him to intervene.

Wasn't going to happen.

He smiled encouragingly and was rewarded by a deep scowl. That was fine. She could be mad as a wet hen. It wasn't going to change anything.

"I already have the water on to boil," Raina insisted. "Besides, I really don't think a cup of tea can be classified as a bother." She led Scout down the hall and out of sight, Samuel following along behind them.

There was a moment of complete silence. Not one word from Jackson or Stella. Not good. Neither of them was known for being quiet.

"Go ahead," he finally said. "Let it out before one of you explodes."

"The only thing I'm going to let out is a yawn," Stella responded. "You think Raina has an extra bed? I'll take the couch if she doesn't. I'll even take the floor if you've got an extra pillow and blanket."

"Upstairs. First door to the right. She made up the bed for you. I told her not to make it too comfortable. You're not used to luxury." Jackson grinned, and Stella swatted him on the shoulder as she walked past.

"Good night, boys. Don't get into any trouble for the next six hours, because I plan on sleeping for at least that long." She walked up the stairs, moving a lot more slowly than usual. Her last mission had taken a toll on her. Physically and mentally.

She'd never admit it, but Boone saw it in her eyes, in the slope of her shoulders, the quick fatigue after minimal work.

He wouldn't say anything. Couldn't. Everyone who'd been on the team for any length of time had had missions that drained them. Stella would come out of it eventually. In the meantime, the team was rallying around her, making sure she didn't do anything stupid while she was recovering.

"Want some coffee?" Jackson asked, already walking down the hall and heading toward the kitchen.

"I'd rather have whatever it is Raina was cooking. It smells great."

"It's some kind of stew. Samuel requested it. Guess he ate it a lot before his parents died." Jackson grabbed a bowl, ladled thick stew out of a stockpot that was sitting on the stove and handed it to Boone. "Spoons are in the—"

"I know where they are." Boone had been in the house on a number of occasions. He'd even celebrated Thanksgiving there. He knew where the silverware was. He also knew where the soda was. He grabbed a can from the fridge and sat at the table.

"Make yourself comfortable," Jackson said drily.

"I have. Thanks."

"Smart aleck," Jackson grumbled as he dropped into the chair across from him.

"Were you expecting something different?"

"Sadly, no. Want to tell me why you decided HEART needed to be involved in this case?"

"For the same reason you got involved in Raina's. I realized someone needed help, and I decided I wanted to be the one to do the helping. HEART has all the resources necessary, and your brother wasn't opposed to using them to bring Lucy home."

"He wasn't enthusiastic about it, either."

"When is Chance ever enthusiastic about anything?" For as long as Boone had known the brothers, Chance had been the more serious one, the more practical. He didn't believe in doing anything based on emotion. He liked rules, and he followed them.

"Good point." Jackson rubbed the back of his neck and frowned. "You said someone ransacked Scout's place. Any idea what they were looking for?"

"None."

"Any idea why someone would go to so much effort to kidnap Scout's daughter?"

"No."

"Do you think *she* knows?"

"I don't know. She was unconscious for three days, and she's not in good enough shape to answer a lot of questions. I'm hoping when she is, she'll have some ideas."

"It might not be a bad idea to push her a little. There's a child missing. Time is of the essence. Scout didn't look great when she walked in here, but she was walking. That's better than a lot of witnesses we've interviewed."

"True."

"So? Why aren't you interviewing her?"

"I plan to. I want to run a couple of things past you first." He scooped up stew and ate it quickly, burning his mouth in the process. Didn't matter. The stuff was good. Lots of spices and chunky pieces of meat and vegetables. "This is good. You're one blessed man, Jackson."

"I'm blessed, but not because Raina can cook. I'm blessed because she's the woman she is and because she's bringing Samuel along with her when she marries me." The sincerity in his eyes was unmistakable. No matter how much Boone liked to jab at the guy, he was happy that Jackson had found someone to love and who loved him in return. That was a great thing, a powerful thing.

When it worked.

And when it didn't, it could cause more heartache than anyone should ever have to experience.

"You're a good guy, Jackson," he said, because it was true. "It pains me to have to say that, because most days I'm not all that fond of you," he added.

"The feeling is mutual. Now that we have that out of the way, how about you tell me what you've found out about Scout?"

"People at work like her. The neighbors like her. She attends church every Sunday and people there have nothing but praise for her. No criminal record. No outstanding warrants. She hasn't had a traffic ticket since she moved to town."

"How long ago?"

"Almost three years."

"Right before her daughter was born?"

"According to her neighbor, she had the baby four months after she moved in."

"Where'd she move from?"

"San Jose."

"That's a long way to come for—what? A job?"

"That's what she told people at her church."

Jackson raised an eyebrow. "You've got a lot of information in a short amount of time. You've obviously been busy."

"Not just me. Stella did a lot of the groundwork while I was at the hospital. The fact that Lucy is missing is opening a lot of mouths that might otherwise be sealed closed."

Jackson nodded. "Does she have family in San Jose?"

"Not that I've found."

"No ex-husband?"

"No record of a marriage or a divorce."

"Then who's the kid's father?"

"Good question. The birth certificate didn't list anyone."

"Interesting." Jackson drummed the tabletop, looking as though he had more to say.

Boone was too impatient to wait for him to think it through. "How so?"

"River Valley is a pretty conservative community. Small-town ideals, you know?"

"I've only been here twice, so I'm not all that familiar with it."

"You grew up in a small town. You know the way things are. People can be judgmental. They like to throw stones while they're living in their glass houses."

"That's a stereotyped view."

"No doubt, but it doesn't change my point."

"Which is?" Boone finished the stew, went back for another helping.

"There are plenty of people around here who would probably be pretty judgmental of a single mother. They'd be watching carefully to see what kind of person she was. One mistake and gossip would fly, people would start murmuring. You haven't heard any murmurs."

"No," he responded, even though it wasn't a question.

"So, we can assume that Scout keeps her nose clean, that she's not out partying every night, probably doesn't have boyfriends who spend the night or druggie pals sleeping it off in her basement."

"What's your point, Jackson?"

"She's living a quiet life, minding her own business, not doing anything that anyone could remotely criticize her for. As far as I can see, there's no one in River Valley who would want to harm her, so we need to be looking a little more closely at her life in San Jose."

"That's what I've been thinking."

"Is that the direction the police are taking?"

"I think they're taking any direction they can find."

"Maybe Chance can put in a call. See what he can find out." Of everyone on the team, Chance was the most diplomatic. He knew how to get the team into areas no one else was allowed, knew how to get information that others would never be given access to, knew how to work the system so that it worked for him.

"You want to ask or should I?"

"Since you're already in the doghouse with him, I'd better do the asking." Jackson stood and stretched. He and Cyrus Mitchell had just returned from a mission to Colombia. The fact that they'd made it back before Thanksgiving was a minor success. The fact that the six teenagers who'd been held hostage at an international school there had been rescued and reunited with their families was a major one. Jackson seemed invigorated rather than worn-out from the trip, riding the high from a successful rescue.

Or maybe he was just riding the high of being reunited with the woman he loved.

Boone wasn't jealous, but he was a little tired of looking into his friend's contented face. He got up and washed his bowl, his back to Jackson. "You put in a call to him, and I'll talk to Scout, see what I can find out about Lucy's father."

"You think she's going to open up to you about it?"

"If she thinks it will reunite her with her daughter," he said as he walked out of the kitchen.

He followed the soft murmur of voices back through the living room and down a narrow hall. There were only two bedrooms there. Samuel's and Raina's. Light spilled out of Samuel's room, and he went there, peering into the open doorway.

Just as she'd promised, Raina had tucked Scout into bed. Or had tried. Scout was sitting on the edge of the mattress, her face pale, what looked like a flannel nightgown in her hand.

"Boone," she said as he stepped into the room, "I'm glad you're here. I was thinking that maybe I should just go back to my place."

"You mean the place that the police don't want you to be?"

"I can't stay here. I'm taking a ten-year-old child's bed." She smiled at Samuel as if she were afraid she'd offended him.

"Samuel is bunking with me," Raina cut in smoothly. "And he's really excited about it. We're going to read and eat popcorn before bed. It's all worked out."

"But—" She tried to protest, but Raina headed for the door.

"Come on, Samuel. I'm going to get Scout some tea,

and you're going to finish your homework. Otherwise, we can't have our reading party."

Take me with you, Scout wanted to say, but they were already gone, their footsteps tapping on the hallway floor as they left her alone in the room with Boone.

He watched her intently, his eyes the deep blue of a midnight sky. He had something to say, and she was afraid of what it was. Had he heard from Officer Lamar? Had something been found? Had Lucy been found?

Her pulse jumped at the thought, and she stood on shaky legs. "Did you hear something from Officer Lamar?"

"No."

"So, they're no closer to finding her." She dropped back on the bed, the jarring movement sending pain shooting through her head. It hurt enough to bring tears to her eyes, but she wouldn't cry. If she did, she might never stop.

"I'm afraid not." He pulled over a child-sized chair and sat in it. He was so tall, they were still nearly eye to eye. "We need to talk, Scout, and I need you to be completely honest with me when we do. Can you do that?"

Could she?

She'd kept her secret for so long, she wasn't sure she could do anything else.

"You're hesitant, but it's the only way I can help you, Scout. If you're not honest, I may as well call my boss and tell him that HEART isn't needed."

"You *are* needed."

"Does that mean you're going to tell me what I want to know?" He didn't smile. As a matter of fact, he had no expression on his face or in his eyes. He could have been talking about taking a walk or going for a drive, could have had absolutely no vested interest in her answer at all.

Maybe he didn't.

Maybe this was just another job to him, and the fact that he was doing it for free made it less important than other jobs.

It was important to her, though.

She needed Lucy. She needed to hear her toddler giggles, listen to her singing in her little-girl voice. Christmas was coming. Scout had planned to put up the Christmas tree and let Lucy help decorate. She'd planned to take her to the live nativity at church, let her pick out gifts to put in a shoe box for Project Christmas Child. She'd had so many plans for this year.

"Scout," he prodded, and she cleared her throat of all the tears she wasn't going to cry.

"I'll tell you what you want to know." She managed to get the words out, and she knew there was no going back. She'd have to answer everything. She'd have to let him see into every dark corner of her life.

He nodded, his face relaxing. "Good. Then let's get started."

SEVEN

She knew what he was going to ask.

She braced herself for it, because she also knew she had to tell the truth, give the name, reveal what she'd never revealed to anyone but Amber.

"Don't look so scared, Scout. I'm not going to use any of the information you give me to hurt you. My only goal is to bring Lucy home."

"Right," she managed to say through a mouth that seemed filled with cotton.

"Then what are you afraid of?" he asked.

"Losing my daughter." That was the truth. It was the reason she'd kept Lucy's paternity to herself. All the other things Amber had warned her about had made her nervous, but losing her daughter? That had terrified her.

"She's already lost," he said gently.

"I know." She swallowed hard, her eyes burning, her heart beating hollowly in her chest. She wanted to go back in time, do something different, *anything* different, to keep Lucy safe.

"Tell me about her father."

"He's not in the picture. He doesn't even know Lucy exists."

"Are you sure?"

Was she? Not really. She didn't think Amber had told anyone about Lucy, but she couldn't be sure and she couldn't ask. "There was only one person who knew who Lucy's father is. She died last year."

His eyes narrowed and he leaned forward. "What happened to her?"

"She committed suicide."

"Did she leave a note?"

"I don't know. I heard about it on the news."

"Okay. Tell you what," he sighed. "How about we stop with the back and forth, and you just tell me the whole story? That'll probably save some time."

"Have you heard of Dale and Christopher Schoepflin?"

"Father and son, right? Both congressmen? I've heard the son might be in line for a presidential nomination."

"My best friend was Dale's daughter, Amber. Christopher is her half brother. He was ten years older than her." This was a lot harder to talk about than she wanted it to be. She hated the story, because it was her story, her mistake, her sin.

That was a hard truth to swallow and a harder truth to speak.

"Amber asphyxiated in her father's garage while he was in D.C. That was pretty big news," Boone said.

She nodded, because she still couldn't believe that her best friend had blocked the tailpipe of her Ford Mustang, turned on the engine and waited to die. The image didn't match with the happy, hyper person she'd grown up with. Amber had been the optimist, the ever-cheerful party girl. If she'd been hiding deep depression, she'd never let on.

"Did you attend the funeral?" Boone pressed for more.

"No, I…" She hesitated, then plunged forward with the information, because hiding it wasn't going to bring Lucy home. "Didn't want Lucy near the family. She's Christopher's daughter."

If Boone was surprised, he didn't let it show. "His wedding was a pretty big deal. I remember seeing pictures of it on magazine covers. When was it? Three years ago?"

"Yes. Two months before Lucy was born." He could figure out the timeline on that, because she wasn't going to go into details.

"He married Rachel Harris, right?"

"That's right." Rachel was a prominent talk-show hostess and an outspoken children's advocate. Scout had never met her in person, but she'd seen her on just about every magazine cover imaginable. The media loved her, because she was beautiful, smart and dedicated to the underprivileged. Her and Christopher's engagement and wedding had ranked right up there with British royalty, and for a while, it seemed it was all anyone had talked about.

"I guess Christopher wouldn't be happy if his wife knew he had a child with someone else," he murmured dispassionately, no judgment or heat in the words.

It didn't matter. Her cheeks were lava hot. She wanted to explain everything. The years she'd wasted on Darren, the way she'd felt when she'd finally realized that he wasn't who he'd claimed to be, the party Amber had invited her to, the secret crush that she'd had on Christopher for so many years it had almost defined who she was.

It seemed like a lifetime ago, and looking back, she could see how gauche she'd been, how naive and easily manipulated. She'd walked right into the perfect firestorm of temptation, and she'd given in to it, because she'd been tired of being the good girl, the good friend, the perfect companion.

"There's no need to be embarrassed," he said, which made her feel only more embarrassed. "This isn't confession time, and it's not about rehashing painful memories. What it's about is finding your daughter. Is it possible that Christopher found out about her?"

"I don't know."

"How about his wife?"

"I don't know that, either. The only one I told was Amber, and I don't know why she'd tell anyone else. She's the one who told me to leave town and warned me not to tell her family about the baby."

"Why?"

"Why what?"

"Why didn't she want you to tell them?"

"She was afraid they'd find a way to take Lucy from me. She was worried that I'd lose custody or that…" She hesitated. Amber's warning had seemed bizarre, her fear out of proportion with the situation. It had been contagious, though, and Scout had never shaken the anxiety her words had brought. "She didn't give me specifics. She just said she wouldn't put anything past them. She was worried that if they couldn't get me to relinquish custody, they might do something to force me into it."

"That could mean anything." Boone's words were light, but his expression was anything but. He looked tough and implacable, all his easy good looks lost in the hardness of his eyes, the toughness of his face.

"She was scared and that scared me. I started looking for a job out of town, and I managed to get an interview here. When they offered me the position, I took it."

"You ran a long way for such a vague threat."

"It didn't seem vague at the time. It seemed like I was doing what I needed to do to stay safe."

"Did you have any contact with Amber after you left? Phone calls? Emails? Texts? Anything that could have been traced?"

"Last year, she sent me two letters and a Christmas gift."

"Do you still have the letters?"

"I did. They were in my filing cabinet in my closet."

"I'll have Officer Lamar look for them. Did you respond?"

"She asked me not to. She said things were…weird." Those hadn't been Amber's exact words, but they were close. Scout closed her eyes, trying to force her brain to remember every detail of the short notes. One in the summer. One in the fall. Then the Christmas gift. Two weeks later, Amber was dead.

Had she planned to take her life when she sent the gift? Had it been some kind of cry for help?

"What are you thinking?" Boone touched her shoulder, and she opened her eyes, realized that he'd leaned closer. There was a faint scar on his cheek, the shadow of a red beard on his jaw. He had the longest lashes she'd ever seen on a man, thick and dark red like his hair. If she'd met him at church, she'd have found him attractive, and she'd have done everything in her power to avoid him.

"That Amber needed me, and I wasn't there for her?" she said honestly, because she'd already told him things she'd never told anyone else, and there didn't seem to be any reason to hide the truth.

He didn't tell her she was wrong, didn't say everything would be okay. "That's a tough thing," he said. "Knowing that you weren't there at the right moment to keep something from happening to someone you love. Me? I've been there. I know the weight of regret. I also know that it doesn't change anything, doesn't help anything."

"What—?"

"It's a story for another time, Scout. Right now, the best thing you can do is stay focused on the present, stay healthy and safe for your daughter's sake. You can make sure that when she comes home, you're able to care for her the way she's going to need to be cared for."

"I know."

"Good. So, you won't try to leave the house tonight? No climbing out the window and trying to get home? No heading off to the accident scene? You won't call anyone, won't ask for any outside help?"

"In other words, no doing anything?" She could have told him right then that wasn't going to happen.

"Exactly. Let us do what we do best and trust that it's going to be enough."

"What if it isn't?"

"I can't tell you that. I can only tell you that what HEART does will be the best anyone can offer, Scout. The rest is up to God." He stood, towering over her, his faded jeans clinging to muscular thighs and narrow hips, his T-shirt clinging to flat abs and broad shoulders. "I'm going to call Officer Lamar and give him the information you shared. He'll probably stop by later to ask more questions, but for now, I suggest you rest."

He walked into the hall before she could respond. Seconds later, Raina walked in. Scout was sure she'd been standing outside the door waiting, but she didn't mention it. Just bustled to the bedside table and set down a cup of tea and a glass of water beside it.

"I brought you some Tylenol." She handed Scout two tablets. "They're not going to do much for the headache, but they may take the edge off the pain. I called the hospital and asked for your discharge instructions. Your doctor wrote a script for pain medication, but you left too quickly to get it. I had the hospital fax it to the clinic where I work. We have a pharmacy there." She spoke almost nonstop as she helped Scout to her feet, pulled back the covers. "How about I help you into that nightgown? You'll be a lot more comfortable sleeping in that."

"I can manage."

"That doesn't mean you should. Did Boone tell you that I'm a nurse? I spent quite a few years working in the E.R."

"No. He didn't."

"I work at a medical clinic now, but I've seen plenty of head injuries. Yours was a serious one. Do too much too soon and you'll end up back in the hospital. I'm not going to push you to take my offer of help, but if you start feeling dizzy or off balance, don't fight through it. Sit down and wait or call for help. Okay?"

"Okay," she agreed, mostly because her legs were shaking and she wanted Raina to leave so that she could sit down again.

"Great. I'll check in on you later." She walked out, closing the door with a quiet click.

Scout dropped onto the bed, popping both Tylenol in her mouth and swallowing them with water. She didn't drink any of the tea. Her stomach was churning, and she wasn't sure she'd keep it down. She didn't bother changing. She wanted to be ready if Officer Lamar showed up. She also wanted to be ready to leave if she decided it was the best option. Right then, she felt too weak to even think about opening the window and doing any of the things Boone had warned her about.

She wanted to do them, though. She wanted to go home, wanted to go to the crash site, wanted to knock on every door in town and demand to look in every house, every room and every closet until she found her daughter.

How much time had passed between the moment she'd been shot and the moment Boone had arrived? Was it enough to have got Lucy out of town or had the kidnappers holed up somewhere to wait until the heat died down?

The police had been looking for three days and they'd found nothing.

She stretched out on the bed, her thoughts racing, her heart racing with them. Three days was a lot of time. Lucy could be anywhere.

If she was even alive.

The thought weaseled its way into her head and wouldn't leave. It pulsed there, screaming for her attention. She didn't want to give it any, because she didn't want to even imagine that she'd never see her daughter again.

She turned on her side, stared out the window, willing herself not to panic. If Amber had been right about her family, it was possible that Christopher had Lucy, that she was safe and being cared for by...

The people who'd tried to kill Scout?

She gagged and had to sit up to catch her breath.

Outside the gibbous moon cast gray-green light on shrubs and grass. It was a pretty yard, set off from any neighbors. On a bluff above it, a light shone through a thick stand of trees. She knew the building that light spilled from. She'd been there once when she'd first moved to River Valley, the little church on the bluff quaint and welcoming. In the end, she'd decided to attend a larger church. She'd wanted the anonymity that came from being in a larger congregation.

She grabbed the chair and dragged it over to the window, pulled the comforter around her shoulders and sat staring out at the night. She didn't want to lie in bed, didn't want to cuddle up under blankets when she wasn't sure if Lucy could do the same.

"Good night, sweet girl," she whispered, wishing those words could drift across the distance between them, settle into her daughter's heart, give her the comfort she needed.

They'd never been apart for more than a few hours. They'd never spent a night without each other. Lucy had to be scared, and thinking about it broke whatever was left whole in Scout's heart.

The house settled around her, the sound of voices slowly dying. The floor creaked above her head. Boone and Jackson settling down for the night? She imagined it must be. Imagined that the doors opening and closing in the hall were Samuel and Raina.

Mother and son?

They looked nothing alike, but the bond between them had been obvious, the young boy's eyes constantly tracking Raina as she moved around the room.

She wanted to know their story, but she wanted Lucy more.

The Tylenol had done little to dull the throbbing in her head, but the aching pain there was nothing compared to the pain in her heart. She had a ten-ton weight on her chest, and if she didn't get up and *do* something, it would crush her.

She crept across the room, opened the door. It didn't creak or groan, but the floorboards gave a little under her feet, the quiet sounds like a soft moan in the darkness.

She didn't know where she was going, but she made her way into the living room and then into the kitchen. Someone had left a light on above the stove, its mellow glow barely illuminating the room. She didn't turn on another light, had no idea what she thought she'd accomplish by being there rather than in the bedroom. She just knew she couldn't sit and wait.

She'd had her purse with her earlier, but she didn't know where it had gone. Her cell phone was in it, and if it still had some charge left in the battery, she could do an online search for Christopher. It had been a while since she'd looked him up. The one night they'd spent together had cured her of the childish crush she'd had. When she'd left the Schoepflin mansion early the next morning, she'd wanted nothing more than to forget what had happened and move on with her life—a little smarter and a whole lot wiser.

She liked to think that she had, but burying her head in the sand, hiding the truth, doing everything in her power to keep Lucy safe hadn't been enough.

She walked back into the living room, looked around for her purse and didn't find it. She'd probably left it in the SUV. She doubted Boone had left it unlocked, but she was just restless enough, just desperate enough to check.

She began easing the bolt open, going slow to avoid unnecessary noise.

"Going somewhere?" Boone said from behind her.

She screamed, whirling to face him.

"What in the world are you doing there?" she gasped.

"What I'm doing is being really unhappy," he muttered, taking her arm and leading her to the couch. "Sit."

She dropped down a little too quickly, her legs weak, her head spinning. "I was looking for my purse."

"I told you to stay inside," he ground out, towering over her. Again. She wanted to tell him to sit down so she wouldn't strain her neck looking up at him, but it would have taken too much effort, so she didn't say anything at all. "You're not going to save your daughter by getting yourself killed," he continued a little more gently.

"Who's going to kill me? You said yourself that no one followed us from my place."

"That's not the point."

"Then what is?"

"You didn't follow the first rule for working with HEART."

"I didn't realize there were rules I had to follow." She squeezed the bridge of her nose. It did nothing to ease her headache. "The fact is," she continued, because he didn't respond, "I couldn't lie in a warm cozy bed while my daughter is missing. I can't close my eyes and sleep when I don't know if she's okay. I don't expect you to understand that, but it is what it is. Until she's home, I have to be working to find her."

Boone eyed Scout, knowing what he needed to say, but not liking it. He didn't talk about Kendal much. Not to friends or family or even fellow members of HEART. He kept his daughter tucked away in a sacred place in his heart that no one was allowed to touch. It was tough, tougher than he'd ever have imagined that it could be, to have a child out in the world somewhere, to be constantly wondering if she was loved, cared for, safe. It ate at a person, and if Boone let himself, he could tumble down deep into depression at the thought of what he'd lost.

That was why he worked so hard, why he kept busy and focused. It was that or lose himself to grief.

"I do understand," he said quietly, and she frowned, her eyes dark with fatigue, the bandage on her head slipping a little to reveal one of many staples that had closed the wound. The bullet had grazed her head, fractured her skull. A millimeter was all that had stood between her and death. If the gunman had adjusted his aim just that fraction of an inch, she wouldn't have survived.

"I doubt it. You think you know. You're trying to understand, but until your daughter is the one missing—"

"My daughter *is* missing," he cut in. "She was taken from me four years ago, and I haven't seen her since."

The words were out, bitter and ugly, but a truth that he hoped would forge a bond between him and Scout. Without her trust, he'd be fighting an uphill battle to keep her safe while he searched for Lucy.

She looked as if she was trying to wrap her head around the words, figure out what they meant in the grand scheme of what was happening to her. "Who took her?" she finally asked. "A stranger? Someone you knew?"

"My wife. I was serving in Iraq, and she left with our daughter. She died of a drug overdose a year later. My daughter wasn't with her."

"Where—?"

"I don't know. I've been all over the country trying to find her, but she's still not home. All I can do is keep looking and pray she's safe, pray she's with someone who loves her and cares for her. *That's* why I joined HEART. It's why I've devoted my life to reuniting families. It's the only reason I do what I do, Scout, because I *do* understand. I've lived it."

"I'm sorry," she said, touching his arm. He felt it like the spring thaw after a harsh winter, the warmth seeping through him, the surprise of it making him look a little more deeply into her eyes.

Her hand dropped away, and she stood. Maybe she'd felt what he had, and maybe she was just as uncomfortable with it as he was.

"I didn't tell you to make you sorry, Scout." He stood, too, stretching a kink out of his lower back and walking to the front door. "I told you because I want you to know that I know what it's like to want to do something even when there is absolutely nothing that can be done. I'll get your purse. You stay in the house. Next time you need something, ask."

He left it at that, walking outside and letting the crisp fall air fill his lungs, clear his head and chase away the memories that were never far from his mind.

EIGHT

Scout didn't sleep. She couldn't. Every time she drifted off, she heard Lucy crying and woke again. Just dreams. She knew that, but her heart jumped every time, her body demanding that she leap out of bed, run from the dream, from the house, from the horrible knowledge that her daughter was gone. By dawn, her eyes were gritty and hot, her body cold and achy. She wanted coffee. Black. She didn't think it would do much to wake her up, but it might chase some of the ice from her veins.

She paced across the room, but didn't open the door. She didn't dare leave the room. She was too afraid she'd run into Boone again. The story he'd told her would have broken her heart if it hadn't already been shattered. She'd wanted to tell him that, but he'd got her purse, handed it to her and escorted her back to the bedroom.

He'd said good-night, and she'd bitten her tongue to keep from asking a dozen questions about his wife, his daughter, the years that he'd spent searching. They were two people who had one terrible thing in common. It didn't make her feel any better to know that someone else had lived through her nightmare, but it did help her understand why Boone was so determined to find Lucy.

Someone knocked on the door, and she hurried to open it, glad for the distraction.

Raina stood in the hallway, a stack of clothes and towels in her hand, her hair pulled back with a pretty blue headband. She wore scrubs and sturdy shoes, and somehow she still managed to look chic and stylish.

"I heard you moving around in here, so I thought I'd peek in before I left for work," she said with a smile. "I brought you some towels and clean clothes."

"I don't want to put you out."

She laughed lightly and thrust the stack into Scout's arms. "Please! Some clothes and towels aren't putting me out any more than the tea I made you last night was. How are you feeling this morning?"

"Like I got run over by a train," she responded honestly.

"I don't doubt it. I want to change that bandage and take a look at the wound, if you don't mind."

"That's not necessary."

"Actually, it is. You don't want an infection to take hold. That can take a person down pretty quickly." She pulled small scissors and gauze from one pocket of her scrubs and rubbing alcohol and cotton balls from the other. "Go ahead and sit down. This will only take a minute. Then you can take a shower and freshen up. There's a new shower cap in the bathroom. I put it on the counter near the sink. It should work to cover your head, but try not to submerse your head." Just like she had the night before, she kept up a running commentary.

Scout gave in and sat, listening to Raina's chatter as the old bandage was eased off her head.

"Hmm," Raina said, dabbing at the skin with an alcohol-soaked cotton ball.

"Hmm what?" Scout glanced in the mirror above the dresser. Did a double take. Sallow skinned with dark circles under her eyes, she had at least two dozen staples from midforehead to her temple. "Good grief! I look like Frankenstein's monster!"

"Not quite." Raina tossed the cotton ball into the trash can and soaked another one.

"Lucy would scream if she got a look at me now."

"Your daughter is three, right?"

"She will be soon. Her birthday is right after Christmas. We were going to have so much fun putting up the Christmas tree and going to the live nativity."

"You'll still be able to do those things."

"They won't be the same if she's not with me."

Raina pressed gauze to Scout's forehead, gently covering the wound. "They won't be, but you'll survive it. You'll learn to get along without, and then when she comes home, you'll be all that much happier to have her with you."

"If she comes home."

"Have a little faith, Scout," she murmured.

"I have plenty of faith."

"Then stop doubting what God can do." She tossed dirty gauze into the trash can, put the rubbing alcohol and extra cotton balls back into her pocket. "I hate to clean wounds and run, but I need to get out of here. Work won't wait. Samuel is still asleep. Hopefully he'll stay that way for a while. If you want coffee, I already started a pot. There's cream in the fridge and sugar in a bowl on the table."

"Thanks," Scout said.

"No problem. If you want some, you should probably get it now rather than later. All bets are off when the boys get back."

"Boys?"

"Men," she laughed. "Boone and Jackson took off about an hour ago."

"I didn't hear them." And she'd been up, pacing the room and listening to the silence.

"They didn't want you to. Boone said they had a meeting with the local police. He probably wanted to weed through the information before giving it to you."

"I'm not sure I like that." As a matter of fact, she was sure she *didn't* like it.

"It is what it is," Raina said calmly. "You're here. You might as well make the best of it. Get a shower. Drink some coffee. Have some breakfast. It could be a busy day today, and you want to be ready for it."

"Of course I do," Scout muttered.

When she saw Boone, she was going to tell him exactly how she felt about being left behind while he went to the police. It wasn't Raina's fault, though, and she didn't want to take her frustration out on her. She tried to smile. "Thanks for the clothes and towels, and thanks for letting me stay here for the night."

"You don't have to thank me, Scout. I was happy to do it. Now, I really do have to get out of here. If you need anything, Stella is upstairs."

She walked into the hall, stood right outside the room. "By the way, I tucked a phone charger in with the clothes and towels. Kind of felt like putting a handsaw in a cake and delivering it to prison, since I'm pretty sure Boone would rather you not have one."

Another thing she didn't like. "He doesn't want me to use my phone?"

"He wants to keep you safe. Cutting you off from the world is the easiest way to do it." She shrugged. "The way I see things, you'll be more likely to stay put if you have some access to the things you want. I'll see you this afternoon." She bustled out of the room, and Scout grabbed the pile of clothes and towels, rifled through them until she found the charger. She plugged in her phone, took a quick shower and dressed in the borrowed jeans and sweater. The jeans were a little loose and a little long. The sweater hung to midthigh. She didn't feel like herself in them. Or maybe she just didn't feel like herself period.

Without Lucy, she didn't know who she was.

Without her, she wasn't sure what to do with her time, how to spend her morning, her afternoon, her evening.

She took the phone and the charger into the kitchen, plugged them in, poured a cup of coffee, went through the motions of a normal day even though nothing about it was normal. She didn't usually take sugar with her coffee, but she scooped in a couple of teaspoonfuls. She hadn't eaten in hours and didn't think she *could* eat, but she needed energy for...

What?

Waiting?

Her phone rang, the sound so unexpected, she jumped.

It rang again, and she scrambled to lift it from the charger, fumbling to hit the right button and answer.

She thought it was Boone, calling to check up on her. "Where are you?" she demanded.

"Shut up and listen," someone hissed, the words chilling Scout's blood. "You want your daughter—you do exactly what I say. Hear me?"

"Yes," she tried to say, but the word caught in her

throat and came out as a breath of air. "Yes," she repeated.

Footsteps pounded behind her and she thought someone had walked into the room, but she didn't turn. She was afraid she'd drop the phone, break the connection, lose her one shot at getting Lucy back.

"Good. You have information I want. I have your kid. We'll do an exchange. What I want for what you want."

"I don't have—"

"I said *listen,*" the caller snapped. A man. She was sure of that. "You have something I want, and if I don't get it, your daughter is mine."

Stella appeared at her side, her red hair wet, her face makeup free. She had freckles—lots of them—and a deep scowl that creased her forehead.

She pulled a chair over and sat, leaning in so that her ear was pressed close to the phone, then grabbed Scout's hand, angling the phone so she could hear.

"You're going to bring me what I want," the caller continued. "And then you're going to get what you want. A nice easy exchange. No drama. No fuss. Understand?"

"Yes, but I don't know what you're talking about. I don't have anything of yours," Scout said, her throat dry, her hand shaking so hard, she almost dropped the phone. Stella tightened her grip on Scout's hand and held it steady, but didn't say a word.

"Don't waste my time, lady. You have it. I want it. You don't know what it is—you'd better figure it out. You've got until midnight tonight. You bring it to the little park near your house. You know the one? You and your kid like to play there."

The fact that he knew that made her numb with fear. "I know it."

"Good. No police. Anyone but you shows up and you'll never see your kid again. Understand?"

"I understand, but I want to talk to Lucy. I want to know she's okay."

The man hesitated, then muttered something that she couldn't hear. She thought she heard a woman's voice, braced herself for the connection to be lost, for any chance she had of speaking to her daughter being lost with it.

"Sixty seconds," the man said abruptly.

She heard shuffling movement, a whimper that made the hair on her arms stand on end. "Lucy?" she said, her voice trembling, her entire body shaking. "Is that you?"

"Mommy!" Lucy wailed, the cry spearing straight through Scout's heart.

"Don't cry, sweetie," she said, tears streaming down her face. She didn't wipe them away. She had sixty seconds, and she couldn't waste even one of them. "Are you okay? Are you hurt?"

"Get me, Mommy." Lucy continued to cry, and Scout wanted to climb through the phone, put her arms around her and hold her close.

"I am. I will. It's just going to take a little more time." Her chest ached, her heart pounding so hard she thought it would fly out. "It's okay. You're okay."

"Get me!"

"I love you, sweetie. I'll be there as soon as I—"

"Time's up," the man cut in, Lucy's cries fading into the background, mixing with the faint sound of a woman's voice. "Tonight at midnight. The park. You bring what I want. I'll deliver what you want. Simple. Easy."

He disconnected.

Scout didn't move, didn't think she was breathing.

Her chest was too tight, her lungs unable to expand. She'd suspected the Schoepflins had something to do with Lucy's kidnapping, but this was worse. A stranger had taken her, wanted to exchange her for something that Scout was sure she didn't have.

"You are not going to panic," Stella growled, taking the phone from her hand and disconnecting the call. "You are not going to fall apart."

Yes, I am, she wanted to say, but Stella glared at her, her eyes hot and angry.

"I texted Boone while you were on the phone. The police are already on this," she continued, every word enunciated and clear as if she didn't think Scout was going to be able to comprehend anything else.

"She was crying." It was all Scout could think of saying. Right at that moment, it was the only thing that seemed to matter. Lucy had needed her, and for the first time in her daughter's life, Scout had failed to bring her comfort.

"I know. I heard," Stella said more gently. "Move past it, okay? You need to focus. The guy said you had something that he wanted. What is it?"

"I don't know." That terrified her, made her breath come faster, her heart race.

"You think you don't. *He* thinks you do. Since he has your kid, I think you'd better figure this out. Think back. Were you given an unexpected gift recently?"

"No."

"Did you bring any books home from the library? Maybe something that had just been reshelved?"

"I brought a bunch of books home last week, but I'm not sure if any of them had just been returned."

"We need to find those and look through them. It's

possible someone tucked information into one of them and you grabbed it before the intended recipient." She was texting as she spoke.

Sending information to Boone?

Scout didn't ask. She felt hollow and empty, Lucy's cries still ringing in her ears.

"Go get your purse," Stella barked. "Grab your coat. Boone will be here in two minutes, and he's taking you over to your place. The police will meet you there."

She tried to jump up, but her body refused anything more than a slow unfolding. She ached. Every bone, every muscle. She hurried to her room, heard the front door open as she grabbed her purse and coat. Boone was there. He'd take her to her house; he'd help her search for the information.

If they didn't find it, what then?

She shrugged into her coat, stumbled back out into the hall, walking right into Boone.

He grabbed her arms, holding her steady. "It's okay," he said.

"No. It's not." But Stella was right. She wasn't going to panic. She wasn't going to fall apart. She was going to search through every inch of her house; she was going to hunt through every book, lift every broken picture frame. She was going to find what she needed, and she had only until midnight to do it.

She hitched her purse up on her shoulder, eased out from Boone's hands. "We need to go. I have no idea what he wants, and I only have a few hours to figure it out."

She walked past him, down the hall, past Stella and Jackson and Samuel, who must have heard the commotion and woken up. She didn't say anything to any of them. Just walked out the door and headed for the SUV that was still idling in the driveway.

They had something to go on. Finally. And Boone had every intention of following up on it. Lamar wouldn't be happy about it. Neither would the FBI agent who'd been at their meeting. They hadn't told him to back off, but they'd made it very clear they could handle the situation themselves.

They could. No doubt about it.

They weren't going to have to.

HEART had plenty of resources and those could be accessed quickly. No bureaucracy, no hoops to jump through. The team decided what needed to be done, and they found a way to do it. Cyrus Mitchell was already working his magic. Lucy's kidnapper had used a cell phone, and Cyrus thought he could follow the signal and pinpoint a location.

If so, they could have Lucy well before the midnight deadline.

He didn't tell Scout that. He didn't want to get her hopes up, and he didn't want her to have any less urgency in the search for whatever it was the kidnapper wanted.

He glanced in the rearview mirror.

Scout sat silently, her body so tense he thought she might snap in two. She hadn't spoken since they'd left Raina's place. Hadn't asked any questions, hadn't mentioned hearing her daughter's voice.

He let her keep her silence. Asking a bunch of questions she couldn't answer wasn't going to help the situation. Stella had filled him in on the conversation and the demands. That was all he needed to know. For now.

He took a straight shot to Scout's place. No side roads.

No worries about being followed. The kidnapper had made his demands known, and the goal was to make him believe those demands were going to be met. Let him see Scout return to her house, let him watch the police and FBI combing the area. The fact that the guy had made his demands by phone just proved that he didn't think he could be caught.

Or maybe he just thought that having a hostage would keep him from being pursued.

It didn't matter.

He'd be caught. HEART had worked cases like this dozens of times. While the FBI and local P.D. went through the proper channels, HEART worked like a well-oiled machine.

He pulled into Scout's driveway, parking behind a squad car. There were several unmarked vehicles, as well, and a uniformed officer stood at the door.

"This should be interesting," he murmured as he offered Scout a hand out.

She didn't take it. Just sat where she was, her face pale, her eyes glassy. She'd been crying, but she'd stopped before he'd arrived at Raina's house.

"Scout," he prodded, touching her fisted hand. "You can't stay here."

"I don't know what he wants." She met his eyes, her gaze hollow and filled with the kind of pain most people would never know. "What am I going to do?"

"You're going to get out of the car." He pulled her to her feet, his hands settling on her waist. "You're going to go inside, and you're going to search the house until you find whatever it is he wants."

"I have never," she whispered, "been so scared of failing in my life."

"You're not going to fail."

"I already did. She was crying for me. She wanted me to come for her, and I couldn't." Her voice broke, but she didn't let any more tears escape.

"That wasn't a failure."

"To Lucy it was. There has never been a time when she's needed me that I haven't been able to be there for her. Until today."

"You'll be with her soon, and she'll forget that you ever weren't."

"You hope."

"I *believe*. There's a difference. Come on." He wrapped an arm around her waist, was surprised when she leaned into him. The subtle shift, the easing of her muscles, the slow melting toward him—it took him by surprise. Since Lana's death, he hadn't had much interest in dating. After experiencing married life, having a child, seeing the beauty of family, he hadn't been interested in playing games. He hadn't wanted short-term, and he'd been sure that he didn't want long-term, either. His life was full of work, of friendships, of a passion for something that most people couldn't understand. He'd dated a few women in the past few years, but he'd known it wouldn't be fair to offer more than one or two dinners, maybe a trip to the movies. He didn't just love his job. He was compelled by it, driven by it. He couldn't *not* do it. Even if he'd wanted to. That left little time for relationships.

That had always been fine by him.

But maybe it wasn't fine anymore.

Maybe he wanted more than his empty apartment and his potted plants. Maybe he wanted someone to go home to.

NINE

She was slogging through mud.

At least, that was how it felt to Scout. She tried to match pace with Boone's long-legged stride, but no matter how much she willed herself to move more quickly, she just couldn't seem to do it.

He must have realized it. He slowed his pace, keeping his arm firmly around her waist as he led her toward a uniformed police officer. If she'd felt stronger, she'd have told Boone she could manage just fine on her own. She didn't. She felt weak and scared. Despite what Boone said, she wasn't sure she'd find what Lucy's kidnapper had demanded. She was hoping that it was in one of the library books she'd brought home. If it wasn't, she had no idea where to look. And if she didn't find it, what would happen? Would she ever see her daughter again?

She gritted her teeth to keep from asking the questions. She knew Boone couldn't give her a definitive answer. He'd said she would be with Lucy soon, said he was believing it rather than hoping it. All the belief in the world couldn't make something true. She'd learned that the hard way.

"Good morning, Ms. Cramer," the officer said, his

gaze jumping from Scout to Boone and back again. "Officer Lamar is waiting for you inside. Your friend is going to have to wait out here."

The muscles in Boone's arm tensed, his fingers pressing a little more firmly into her side. He didn't speak, though, didn't argue. She could have walked inside and left him where he was. It should have been the easy thing to do. She'd been going it alone for so many years that she'd forgotten what it was like to have someone in her corner.

Until Boone had come along, and suddenly she remembered how it felt to stand shoulder to shoulder with another person, to know there was someone to hold her up when she wanted to fall down. She didn't want to give that up.

"I'd rather he come with me," she said, and his fingers caressed her waist, smoothing along the edges of her waistband in a subtle sign of approval.

"Sorry. That's not possible."

"Why not?" Boone asked without heat or aggression. He might have been asking the time of day or commenting on the weather, for all the emotion in his voice.

"The house is a crime scene. We're still processing it."

"I don't think so," Boone said with a smile that looked more feral than polite. "I was in Officer Lamar's office earlier this morning. He made it very clear that Scout could return home. Would he have done that if he was still processing the scene?"

"I don't—"

"We both know that he wouldn't," Boone continued. "So, what's the problem?"

"The FBI is already working with the River Valley P.D. We don't need a third party involved."

"I'm here as Scout's friend. Are you going to deny a crime victim the support she needs?"

"We're doing everything in our power to make this as easy on Ms. Cramer as we can."

"You didn't answer my question," Boone pointed out.

The officer scowled. "Stay here. I'll check with Lamar. If he says you're in, you're in. If he says you stay out, you're out."

He walked inside, closing the door just a little too firmly behind him.

"Nice guy," Boone said easily.

"He probably is. Most days."

"Just not today?" Boone asked with a half smile. He seemed distracted, his eyes scanning the yard, the driveway, the copse of trees across the road.

"What are you looking for?" she asked, and his ocean-blue gaze landed right smack-dab on her face. She'd thought he was handsome the day they'd met, but she hadn't realized how handsome. The angle of his jaw and cheekbones, the firm curve of his lips, the day's growth of beard on his chin created a picture that nearly stole her breath.

"Someone affiliated with the guy who took your daughter. He wasn't working alone. More than one car followed you from the store the night Lucy was taken. I'd say that he's got someone watching the house, making sure you're looking for whatever it is he wants."

She tensed, the thought of someone watching her, stalking her while she searched, making her skin crawl. "We should tell the police."

"They know. The FBI knows. This is something we've all done dozens of times. Every kidnapper thinks he's unique, but most of them are working under the same premise. They want something. They make sure they have something valuable to barter with. In this case, Lucy. Once they have that, they aren't content to sit and wait. Most of the time, they're actively keeping tabs on the victim's family."

"Nice." She shivered, and he shrugged out of his jacket, draped it around her shoulders. It smelled like soap and aftershave, and she burrowed in, letting his warmth seep into her.

"*Predictable* is a better word," he responded. "See the guy in your living room window?" He eased her around so she was facing the house.

Sure enough, someone was standing in front of the window. "Yes."

"He's doing the same thing I am—looking for someone who's hanging around watching you."

"I'm not sure I like the idea of someone skulking around keeping tabs on me."

"The guy who called you is going to want to know that you're following orders. He'll be happy to see that things are going exactly the way he wants. It's nothing to worry about."

"I'm not worried about him watching me. I'm worried that I won't be able to find what he wants by the midnight deadline. I have limited time, and I'm standing outside my house waiting."

"It's your house, Scout. If you want to be inside, go inside."

"The officer—"

"Can't keep you from your property. Lamar cleared it as a crime scene last night. That being the case, he can't keep you outside."

"I've never been much of a rebel, Boone. I can't imagine doing something a police officer told me not to do."

"There's a first time for everything." He reached past her, turned the doorknob. The door swung open, revealing her still-trashed living room and a group of men and women who seemed to be in the midst of a heated discussion. They went silent as Boone nudged her across the threshold.

"Sorry to break up the party," he said. "But we're on a time crunch here, and Scout is feeling a little stressed about it."

"The last thing I want," Officer Lamar said as he separated himself from the group, "is to cause you any more stress than you've already had, Scout. But we really need to conduct this search in an organized manner. The best way to do that is to limit the number of people in the house." He sent a pointed look in Boone's direction.

She ignored it.

"I'll make sure not to invite anyone else. If you don't mind, I'm going to look at the library books I checked out last week." She grabbed Boone's hand without thinking, tugging him past the group and into the narrow hall. They made it all the way to her bedroom before he pulled her to a stop.

"What?" She met his eyes, her cheeks heating when he smiled.

"I'm impressed, Scout," he said, his Southern drawl deep and rich. If she heard it every day for the rest of her life, she didn't think she'd get tired of it. "I can't say I've ever seen a conformist rebel quite so well."

"I never said I was a conformist." She tugged away, because heat was shooting up her arm, swirling in her belly, and she didn't have time to think about what that meant or to decide if she wanted to explore it more.

"Seems to me that you probably are. You live a quiet life, doing quiet things that don't bother anyone. I talked to your neighbors, your coworkers, your church family. Not one person had a bad thing to say about you."

"First, you make that sound like a bad thing. Second, I'm not all that happy about the fact that you were talking to people I know."

"You were unconscious and your daughter was missing. Would you rather I waited until you came to to figure out if you might have had someone in your life who was capable of taking Lucy?"

"I'd rather none of this had happened," she responded, stepping into her room.

It looked the same as it had the day before, the mess somehow magnified in the watery light that streamed through the window. She walked to the bookshelf that usually housed the library books she brought home for the week. All ten of the books were on the floor, jackets torn off, spines broken. She'd have to pay for them, but that didn't matter. What mattered was that they'd already been searched. She could see that. Should have thought of it before.

Deflated, she knelt beside them, lifting the one closest to her. The pages were bent, the cover torn off and ripped apart. "The books have already been searched."

"Did you hang your hat on the idea that you'd find something in one of them?" Boone picked up another book, flipped through the pages several times.

"Stella thought maybe that's how I'd got whatever it is the kidnapper wanted. She said I might have brought it home in a library book."

"It was a good idea," he said gently, taking the book from her hand and setting both on the shelf. "But sometimes even the best ideas don't work out."

"I…" *…just wanted to think that it would.* She lifted another book, shook it out and set it with the others, her heart too heavy to continue. She hadn't hung her hat on the idea, but she'd wanted so badly to walk in and find what she'd been looking for. "Don't know where else to look."

"Did you buy anything recently? Furniture? Computer? Something used that someone might have hidden something in?"

"No. I was waiting until after Christmas to do my shopping. Lucy has grown so much this year, and she needs new everything." Her voice wobbled and she knew that if she didn't do something, she was going to cry again. She stood, walked to her closet and the file cabinet. It had been emptied, of course, and she sifted through the tax documents and receipts, looking for the letters Amber had sent. They weren't there.

She frowned, lifting the cabinet and looking under it.

"Are you looking for Amber's letters?" Boone asked as he grabbed the mattress and tossed it back on the bed.

"They aren't here."

"You're sure?" He stopped, both of her pillows under his arms. It looked as if he was trying to make up the bed, and for some reason, that touched her heart.

"They're not with the rest of the things that were in here, but there's stuff strewn all over the room, so maybe I just haven't found them yet."

He frowned, tossing the slashed pillows on top of the mattress. "I need to know for sure. If those letters were taken, that provides a direct link to the Schoepflin family."

"What does?" Officer Lamar walked in, a woman in a dark suit following him.

"I got some letters from Amber Schoepflin before she died. They're missing."

"Interesting," the woman said. "I'm Special Agent Lynette Rodriguez. My team and I are working with Officer Lamar to bring Lucy home. We've already sent an agent to talk to Christopher Schoepflin. He's denied any involvement in this but will be flying in from California tomorrow to meet with us."

She nodded, because she didn't know what to say.

There was nothing *to* say. When Christopher arrived, she'd have to explain to him. At that moment, she couldn't make herself care. All she wanted was to have Lucy back. Everything else could be worked out after that. Whatever mistakes she'd made, she could rectify them. Whatever wrongs she'd committed, she could apologize for. She couldn't go back in time and change her decision, but she could make better ones in the future.

If she had the chance. If Christopher hadn't been involved in kidnapping Lucy.

"What we'd like to do today," Agent Rodriguez continued, "is look for two things. The letters you've said are missing and whatever it is the kidnapper wants."

"I have no idea what that is," she admitted, and the agent nodded.

"Let's go sit in the kitchen. We'll make a list of possibilities."

She didn't like the idea, especially because Officer Lamar had pulled Boone aside and was speaking quietly to him. She couldn't hear what he was saying, and that bothered her. It was as if they had a secret they were trying to keep from her.

Boone must have sensed her hesitation. He met her eyes. "Go ahead. I'll be there as soon as I can, and I'll fill you in on what we discuss."

She didn't normally take someone's word on blind faith. Not anymore. Darren had told her that they'd get married, have a family and build a life together. He'd ended up running off with his sister's best friend. Christopher had whispered a thousand sweet promises in her ear. He'd told her that she was beautiful and sweet and that he'd never realized just how much he was missing out on. He'd promised that they wouldn't just have one night, that every night would be special. By the next day, he'd decided that he'd made a mistake, that Rachel really was the woman he wanted.

Scout had been devastated. Again.

She didn't plan to repeat the mistake. She wasn't going to put her trust in someone who wasn't trustworthy.

But Boone? She believed him. Maybe she even believed *in* him, because she trusted that he'd do everything he could, spend every hour he had available trying to bring Lucy home.

"Scout," the agent urged. "We really do need to get this list made. In cases like yours, time is of the essence."

"Right," she said, turning away from Boone and following Agent Rodriguez into the kitchen.

Three hours, fifteen minutes and thirty seconds.

That was how long Boone and Officer Lamar spent searching the house for the letters Amber had written. They looked in every closet, looked under every piece of furniture. They checked under throw rugs and in the trash can. No sign of the letters.

"Someone took them," Lamar growled as he dropped a basket full of clothes on the floor of Scout's tiny laundry room. There was just enough space in the room for one adult, but somehow Lamar had maneuvered his way in. Boone wanted to tell him to back out, but he didn't want to butt heads with the guy. Not when they were working toward the same goal.

"It looks that way. Although, with the mess the perps left, it's possible we missed it."

"We didn't miss it." Lamar smoothed his hair and grimaced. "First time in my career as a police officer that I wish I'd been wrong about something."

"Wrong about what?"

"The Schoepflins. I was hoping we wouldn't find a connection between them and the kidnapping. Too much hassle involved in pretending diplomacy to appease their high-class sensitivities. I'd much rather forget about them and look in another direction."

"What direction would that be? Drugs? Money?"

"Who knows?" Lamar shrugged. "Scout could have walked into any number of scenarios. She could have seen something, heard something. Plenty of innocent people get pulled into trouble that way. Not that it matters. At this point, with those letters missing, I'd say the Schoepflins are the direction we need to look. I just hope it leads us to the kid. I have a daughter of my own, and I don't like the idea of a toddler out there in the world with a stranger."

"Any luck tracking the cell phone that was used to call Scout?"

"Not yet. The FBI is working on it." He paused. "How about your team? And don't tell me they're not trying."

"As far as I know, we've come up empty." Though he was pretty sure Cyrus was getting close. He expected to get a call at any moment, and when he did, he was moving out. Nothing was going to keep him from going wherever that cell phone signal had come from.

"I'm expecting that the FBI will locate the signal before your people do. Don't mess things up for them, Anderson. Don't try to go maverick and save the kid on your own. We don't need a hero—we need a live child to bring home to her mother."

"Your assumptions are insulting. I may work in the private sector, but I'm not doing it for the glory. Fact is," he said, keeping his tone neutral, because Lamar looked as though he was pushing for a fight and Boone wasn't in the mood to take him up on it, "there isn't any glory involved in what I do. You ever see any of our team members talking to the press, building up HEART to get more clients?"

Lamar scowled and didn't respond.

"Of course you don't, because that's not why we do what we do. Now, if you'll excuse me—" he brushed by Lamar "—Scout's probably wondering where I am."

"Hold on a minute," Lamar called.

Boone ignored him.

He'd done his part. He'd played nice. He'd followed the rules and walked around the house looking for something he'd known they weren't going to find. He was done. Time to get things moving along.

He walked into the kitchen, saw Scout sitting at the kitchen table alone. She had deep shadows under her eyes and hollows beneath her cheekbones, but she smiled when she saw him, and his heart jumped in response.

"Hey," she said. "I was wondering when you were going to show up."

"Sorry it took so long. I got sidetracked." He sat beside her. "Where's Agent Rodriguez?"

"She got a call a few minutes ago and walked out back. I don't want to get my hopes up, but I've been sitting here wondering if maybe they've found Lucy. I've even been thinking about what I'm going to do when I finally get my hands on her again. Thinking about all the hugs and kisses that I'm going to give her." She scraped at a little spot on the table and frowned. "That's probably stupid, isn't it? I should probably be preparing for the worst."

"No." He covered her hand with his, waited until she met his eyes. "Stupid would be giving up hope."

"What is hope except the belief in something that you desperately want but aren't sure is going to happen?" She stood and paced to the window above the sink, her slim body nearly shrouded by jeans and an oversize sweater. "It seems useless. Like sitting at a kitchen table answering dozens of questions about things that probably have nothing to do with my daughter's disappearance."

"What kind of questions are we talking about?" he asked, curious about the direction the FBI was heading. More than likely, they were trying to rule Christopher out. Or rule him in.

"We went over every delivery I've received in the past year. We talked about my friends, my work. She wanted to know about Amber, too. I told her about the letters. Funny, I'd put them out of my mind until all this happened."

"Yeah?" He moved up behind her, turned her so that they were facing each other. She looked tired, weary, discouraged—all the things he'd seen in all the faces of the waiting and wondering. He wanted to tell her that everything would be fine, that Lucy would come home to her and that they'd go on the way they had before. He couldn't. Not if he were going to be honest.

"Were you friends for long?" he asked instead.

"Forever. She was like a sister to me. I hadn't thought about that in a while, either." She smiled, but the sadness in her eyes was unmistakable. "You know how it is when you meet someone and you just know you're going to be friends forever? That's how it was with me and Amber. We were completely opposite of each other and completely the same."

"I've never had someone like that in my life," he said honestly.

"I'm almost as sorry for you as I am for myself, then." She walked past him, filled a kettle and set it on the stove to boil. "I don't suppose you're a tea drinker? All my coffee got dumped. I guess whoever ransacked my house thought I might be hiding something in with it."

"No tea, but if you've got anything to eat around here, I'd be grateful."

She laughed a little and pulled a box of animal crackers from the cupboard. "They didn't dump these. I guess because the box was sealed, they didn't think I'd hidden anything in it."

"Perfect." He tore open the box and took a handful. He imagined they were what she gave Lucy as a treat, but he didn't mention it. She looked wounded enough, and he didn't want to add to that. "Did you give Agent Rodriguez the gift Amber sent you?"

"She didn't ask for it. It was just a Christmas-tree ornament. A glittery pink frame with a photo of us when we were kids in it. I kept it in the living room for a while, but Lucy loved it and always tried to get her hands on it. I finally just put it in a box with the rest of the Christmas stuff."

"Where's that?" he asked, snagging another handful of crackers and handing one to her.

"My landlady has a storage unit. She let me keep a few things there."

"Do you have access to the unit?"

"Yes. I have a key to the lock and the combination to the front gate."

"Agent Rodriguez didn't ask for it?"

"She did, but she seemed more interested in the letters. She asked me what Amber said, if there was anything unusual in them. There wasn't."

He nodded, but his mind was circling back to the picture frame. "I was thinking that maybe you want to decorate for Christmas before Lucy gets home." He took a few more crackers. "I can send Jackson out to get that box for you, and he can bring it over here."

"I'm not in a holiday mood," she said wearily, putting the cracker he'd handed her back in the box and taking a tea bag from a small box in the cupboard. She poured water over it even though he doubted it was much more than lukewarm.

"I don't need you to be in the mood for it. I just need you to give me the information so that I can send Jackson to get the box."

"If that's what you want, go for it." She grabbed a scrap of paper from a pile on the counter, found a pen in a drawer and jotted the information down for him. He fig-

ured the FBI was already checking things out, but he made
the call to Jackson anyway. He was just finishing the call
when Agent Rodriguez walked in.

She didn't look happy.

"I've got some unpleasant news," she said without
preamble.

"Is it Lucy?" Scout asked, her face losing every bit of
color. He slipped an arm around her waist, felt her whole
body shaking. Was surprised when her hand settled on
his side, her fingers clutching the fabric of his shirt.

"No. Sorry. I should have made that clear from the
beginning." Rodriguez frowned.

"Yeah, you should have," Boone retorted, not happy
with how pale Scout looked, how weak she seemed to
be. He knew what it was like to wait, knew the helpless feeling, the desperation. Knew how easy it was to
forget things like sleep and food. She hadn't eaten the
animal cracker. Had she eaten anything since she'd left
the hospital?

"We all make mistakes, Mr. Anderson. I've made my
apology, so how about we get back to business? I spoke
with the medical examiner who autopsied Amber Schoepflin's body. He ruled suicide because of the circumstances
Amber was found in, but he noted some bruising on her
arms and a needle mark that was consistent with an in-
jection. Toxicology reports showed that she had a high
level of heroin in her body."

"Amber didn't take drugs." Scout frowned. "She didn't
even like taking Tylenol."

"That's what her family said, but the circumstances
were indicative of suicide and the M.E. ruled accord-
ingly. With everything that's happened, I've asked for
her case to be opened again. I want the San Jose po-

lice to take a closer look at what she was doing before she died, because I don't think she committed suicide. I think she was murdered."

TEN

A million questions. That was what Agent Rodriguez was asking. Scout wasn't able to answer many of them. She knew that Amber had been working as a reporter for the local paper, that she'd loved to party but never drank to excess. She knew that she'd broken up with her boyfriend and had been dating someone new in the months before her death, but she couldn't remember the guy's name and wasn't even sure Amber had ever mentioned it.

"How many times did you speak to Amber after you left San Jose?" Agent Rodriguez didn't seem to be wearing down, but Scout sure was.

She rubbed the back of her neck, trying to ease the tension there. "Not many. She was always afraid her family was listening in on the conversation."

"Why would they do that?"

"Because they were crazy that way? That's what Amber always said. I don't know what she meant. I didn't spend all that much time at her father's place."

"Did she—?"

"You know what?" Boone interrupted. "I think you've asked enough questions. Scout is still recovering, and she needs her rest."

"Which does she need more? Rest or her daughter's return?"

"If answering your questions could bring her daughter back, she'd be standing in this room right now."

"This is all part of the process," Agent Rodriguez argued. "By gathering the facts, we can narrow down our search area."

"Is there a search area?" Scout asked, because it seemed as if nothing was being done. It seemed as if they were spending all their time in the kitchen, discussing something that had happened a year ago while her daughter got ready to spend another night without her.

"Yes," Agent Rodriguez assured her, but she doubted it was true. How could it be? Not only did they not know who had Lucy, but they had no idea where to look to find her.

"I'm supposed to meet with the kidnapper at midnight. I need to—"

"You may as well know up front that that meeting is not going to happen." Agent Rodriguez cut her off. "It would be too dangerous, and the likelihood that your daughter will be at the park tonight is slim to none."

"You can't keep me from going," she responded, standing so quickly, her head spun.

"Actually, I can. It may be your daughter who's missing, but this is my case, and I can't have you interfering. You try to go, and I'll have my officers detain you."

"So, I'm just supposed to sit here and wait for the deadline to pass?"

"Unfortunately," Agent Rodriguez said, "yes."

The room seemed to close in around her, and Scout's chest hurt so badly, she thought she might be having a heart attack. She wanted to scream, to rant, to rage against everyone and everything that was keeping her from her daughter. She couldn't. She didn't have Amber's strength or Boone's courage. She was just herself, a little meek, a little quiet. Darren had called her mousy, and she hadn't been all that offended, because mousy was how she usually felt.

Right then, she just felt suffocated. "I need some air," she muttered.

She didn't wait for permission, just ran out the back door, raced across the little yard that she and Lucy had spent so much time in. She'd made it to the edge of the trees at the back of the property when Boone caught up. He pulled her to a stop, his hand wrapped around hers, his palm warm and just a little rough.

"Next time, wait for me," he said.

"I couldn't breathe," she responded. "I really couldn't." Her voice broke, and all the tears she'd been holding back, all the fear and anxiety and anger burst out. She cried as if the world had ended, because she thought that maybe it had.

"Shh," he said, pulling her into his arms. He smelled like fresh air and sunshine mixed with something masculine and just a little dark, and she wanted to burrow into him, stay there until the nightmare ended and Lucy was home. "You're okay."

"No. It's not," she sobbed. "Lucy is missing, and all I'm doing is sitting at my kitchen table, having tea and answering questions."

"I didn't say *it* was okay. I said *you* were." He eased back, cupping her face in his hands, his eyes dark blue and filled with compassion. "There's a big difference, Scout. One you have no control over. The other you do."

"I don't have any control over any of it—that's the problem." She stepped away, swiping at the tears.

"You know what I've realized during the years my daughter's been missing?" he asked quietly, his hair gleaming in the afternoon sunlight, his eyes deeply shadowed. "We don't always have to be in control to be content. We don't always have to know every outcome to have peace. Sometimes we've just got to trust that the things we can't control are in God's hands, that He's working His good through the worst of circumstances."

Coming from anyone else, it would have sounded clichéd and trite, but Boone had lived her nightmare. He knew every ache of her heart. "I wish I had your faith. I wish that I could believe something good was going to come out of this."

"I wish I had my daughter," he responded. "But I don't, and because I don't, I'm helping you find yours."

"It's not a fair trade. Not for you."

"Nothing about life is fair." He smoothed loose strands of hair from her cheek, his hand settling at her nape, kneading muscles that were taut from nerves and fear. "But I think you already know that."

She nodded, her heart pounding in her ears, butterflies dancing in her stomach. His hand felt warm and wonderful, and that scared her more than she wanted to admit. She'd made a big mistake with Christopher, her silly childhood crush allowing her to believe all the sweet lies he'd whispered to her. She'd given up everything she'd believed in so she could believe in him.

She wouldn't make that mistake again.

She moved away, cold air cooling her heated cheeks.

"What I know is that you didn't have to help me the night of the accident, and you did. You've been helping me ever since, and I don't know how I'm ever going to repay you." That was the truth. Everything else—the butterflies in her stomach, the connection that seemed to arc between them when she looked in his eyes—didn't matter.

"I'm not doing this for payment. I'm doing this to bring your daughter home." He raked a hand through his hair and sighed. "So, do me a favor. No more running outside when the mood strikes, okay?"

She couldn't promise that. If she thought it would bring Lucy home, she'd run straight toward a firing squad. "I don't—"

Something snapped in the woods behind them, the sound echoing on the still air and chilling Scout's blood.

One minute, she was standing, and the next, she was on the ground, Boone lying on top of her, the weight of his body pressing her into the loamy earth. She twisted, trying to see if something was coming. If some*one* was coming.

"Don't move," he whispered, his breath tickling the hair near her ear.

The world had gone still, the day silent. No birds chirping in the trees. No animals scurrying in the underbrush. Nothing but her quick panting breaths. "What—?"

"Shh," he murmured. "Listen."

She did. Silence. Then the soft crunch of leaves, barely audible, but there. Someone was coming, and her muscles tightened with the need to run. She wanted to spring from the ground, race back to the house, hide under a bed or in a closet, but Boone had her pinned to the ground, his weight crushing the breath from her lungs. Or maybe it was fear that was doing that.

She could feel the thud of his heart through her shirt,

feel his muscles contract as the footsteps stopped. "Listen to me," he breathed. "We've got a line of underbrush separating us from whoever is there. As long as you stay low, you're gold. Understand?"

She nodded, because she couldn't catch enough air to breathe, and because anything she might have wanted to say was trapped in the lump of terror that clogged her throat.

"Good. I'm going to check things out. Stay here until I get back or until Lamar or Rodriguez comes to escort you to the house."

His weight lifted, and she could breathe again, think again, and what she was thinking was that they should both stay right where they were and let the FBI or the police find whoever was skulking through the woods.

"Boone, wait!" she whispered as he eased into the foliage.

He looked back, his ocean-blue eyes blazing in the afternoon sun. He didn't look like the man who'd held her when she'd cried. He didn't look like the guy who'd eaten handfuls of animal crackers from the box. He didn't look like the grieving father still searching for his daughter. He looked...dangerous, deadly.

"Stay here and stay down and stay silent." The words were clipped, his tone dead of all emotions. He turned away, slid into the thick undergrowth, barely rustling the leaves as he moved.

She lay where she was, counting silently in her head. Sixty seconds. One hundred and twenty. No one exited the house. Nothing moved in the woods, but the birds were silent, the afternoon eerily quiet. Thick bushes and brambles butted up against her yard, dead fall leaves covering the ground. She'd hear someone coming, wouldn't she?

And if she did, then what?

Would she lie still like Boone had said?

Run for the house?

Fight?

The police were in her house; the FBI was there. Someone had to be aware of what was happening. Didn't they?

She reached in her pocket, pulling out the cell phone she'd stuck there. She'd been carrying it everywhere, because she hadn't wanted to miss a call from the kidnapper.

Stay here and stay down and stay silent!

That was what Boone had demanded she do, but what if there was more than one person in the woods? What if Boone was ambushed because she'd stayed silent and complacent? She couldn't live with that. She had to call 911, make sure that the men and women in the house knew what was happening outside.

The phone buzzed, and she nearly dropped it in surprise. She glanced at the caller ID. Anonymous.

She knew who it was.

Knew that the man who had her daughter was calling her again. She had to answer. She didn't care if someone heard her talking or took a shot at her because of it.

"Hello?" she said, her voice trembling, her body stiff and tense. She expected a gunshot, expected to feel the pain of a bullet piercing her flesh.

"Tell your friend to back off."

"I don't know what you're talking about," she lied, because she wanted to buy time, give Boone a chance to catch up to whoever it was he was hunting.

"You tell him he's in my crosshairs. Tell him he keeps coming and he's not going to live to see another day.

Maybe he won't care so much about that, but he's not the only one on the wrong end of the barrel. First him. Then your kid."

Then the phone went dead.

It was a trap. She was almost certain of it, but she couldn't *not* go after Boone. Not just for Lucy's sake. For his, because he'd done so much and asked so little, and because he deserved more than to die in a cold forest on the outskirts of River Valley.

She jumped up, plunged into the woods, branches breaking, twigs snapping. Behind her, someone shouted, but she didn't stop. She could lose Boone and Lucy, and the fear of that was greater than the fear of being kidnapped, wounded or killed.

Branches snapped, twigs broke, the sounds reverberating through the forest as Boone stepped across a small creek and climbed the steep embankment on the other side. He paused at the top, crouched low as he listened. Someone was coming, and he wasn't being quiet about it.

Not the guy Boone was tracking. That was for sure.

He was up ahead. Close enough that Boone had caught a glimpse of him scrambling over the embankment.

Running scared, and he should be. The Feds had already set up a roadblock to keep anyone from entering or exiting the country road that wound through the sixty-acre park that Scout's property backed onto.

If the perp had parked there, he'd be caught before he made it to the main road.

If he hadn't, he'd be traveling a long way by foot before he could get to his vehicle. Stella was on that, checking parking areas and neighborhoods that butted up against the park. No doubt the local P.D. and Feds were doing the same.

He stepped behind a tall spruce, the boughs shielding him from whoever was following. More twigs snapped; feet splashed through water. Feet and hands scrambled on dirt, and Boone could hear rocky earth falling into the creek. Finally, his pursuer made it up the embankment.

Boone didn't wait. Didn't even hesitate. He had limited time to get this job done, to dispatch his pursuer and get back to hunting the guy he was pursuing.

He lunged from his cover, saw dark blond hair a moment before he made contact.

Scout!

He rolled onto his back to keep from crushing her as they fell, grabbed her arms as she tried to fight him off.

"Cool it!" he hissed, so angry he could barely get the words out.

"Boone?" She stopped struggling, looked up into his face with such abject relief that some of his anger faded away.

"Lucky for you," he spat, all his frustration seeping out in the words. "Didn't I tell you to stay put?"

"I got a call from Lucy's kidnapper. He said he had you in his crosshairs and that if you didn't back off, he was going to shoot you. He said Lucy was next." She was out of breath, the bandage that had covered her wound gone, exposing staples from the middle of her forehead to her temple.

"You could have been first." He pulled her to her feet. "Did you think of that before you came tearing out into the woods?"

"Yes." She raised her chin a notch, her eyes blazing. "And I decided you and Lucy were worth the risk."

What could he say to that?

It made sense, and he knew that if he'd been in her position, he'd have done the same.

"Here's the thing," he said, trying to tamp down the frustration that was hammering away at his chest. "I was an army ranger before I joined HEART. I know how to track someone without becoming his victim. I know how to bring someone down without making a sound. You—" he shook his head, because he still couldn't wrap his mind around what she'd done "—are a librarian."

"What does that have to do with anything?" she demanded.

"You aren't trained for this. You know nothing about it. You came running through the trees making enough noise to wake the dead. In a situation like this, that's a surefire way to get yourself killed!"

"I did that on purpose," she protested. "To distract the kidnapper."

If the situation hadn't been so serious, he would have laughed. "Did you really think he was going to be distracted?"

"What I thought," she said quietly, all her defensiveness gone, nothing left in her eyes but emptiness and loss, "was that you and my daughter were in danger and if I had to sacrifice myself to save you both, I would."

That hit him harder than it should have. He'd worked with plenty of men and women in the military who'd have given their lives for a comrade. He'd found the same in his buddies at HEART. But out in the great wide world where ordinary men and women lived ordinary lives doing ordinary things, it wasn't often he ran into someone willing to risk everything for those she loved.

"That's admirable," he said gently, taking her arm

and leading her back toward the embankment. "But you being dead won't keep me or your daughter from dying. Remember, the guy who kidnapped Lucy believes you have something he wants. Since it wasn't in your house, he's going to need you to find it. More than likely, he was trying to flush you out, get you away from the safety of the people who are trying to protect you."

"And I was walking right into his trap?"

"You were running," he corrected. "Loudly."

She smiled at that, but there was still a hint of sadness in her eyes and a whole bucketload of loss. "And with purpose. For the record, I knew that I was probably heading into a trap, Boone. I just didn't care. I figured if I was kidnapped, maybe they'd bring me to Lucy. If I was killed..." She shrugged. "Anyway, I may just be a mousy little librarian, but I'm not stupid."

"Mousy? I don't recall saying anything about that," he said as he walked along the edge of the embankment.

"You didn't have to," she responded, following so closely behind him, they might as well have been one person. "I know what I am."

"I don't think you do," he responded. "Because from where I'm standing, you are beautiful, interesting, kind. That's a pretty heady combination for a guy like me," he said honestly, because he'd never been the kind of guy to beat around the bush. When he wanted something, he went after it. When he thought something, he said it. When a woman intrigued him, he didn't see any reason to hide it.

And Scout *did* intrigue him.

"What kind of guy is that?" she asked.

"One who is just trying to make the best of the hand he's been dealt."

"You do more than that," she said softly, and he glanced over his shoulder, met her eyes.

"Some days I think I do. Some days, I'm not so sure. This spot looks good. I'm going to climb down. Then I'll give you a hand."

"I can—"

"Scout," he interrupted. "You may intrigue me, but you also irritate the living daylights out of me. Please, can we just skip the argument so I can get you back to the house and get back to my search?"

"You're not going to keep chasing the guy, are you?" she asked, and he sighed, dropping down over the side of the embankment. He landed on soft moist earth, then reached up to help Scout down when something moved in his periphery. Not something. A man. Slipping out from between the trees.

"Get down, Scout!" Boone yelled, pivoting and pulling his gun in one smooth motion.

ELEVEN

Scout dropped to the ground, expecting the world to explode in a barrage of gunfire, expecting that everything she'd been hoping to avoid by running into the woods was about to happen.

"Hold your fire!" a man called, and she lifted her head, looked down into the creek bed.

"Are you nuts, Mitchell?" Boone growled. "You about near got your head blown off."

"When have you ever fired a gun without knowing exactly what you were going to hit?" the man asked, stepping out from the shadow of the trees.

"Good to know you've got so much confidence in me, but I'd have rather you let me know you were out here." Boone reholstered his gun.

"Kind of hard to do when you said you wanted radio silence." Mitchell looked up, his dark eyes settling on Scout. "You must be Scout."

"Yes."

"Cyrus Mitchell. With HEART."

"Nice to meet you," she said, scrambling to her feet and wondering how she was going to get into the creek bed without tumbling onto her butt.

"Just shimmy over the edge," Boone said as if he knew exactly what she was thinking. "It's only ten feet. I'll help you to the ground."

"Okay. Sure." Except that ten feet looked a whole lot more like twenty when you were standing on the top of it.

"Are you really going to start doubting me now?" Boone sighed. "I'll come up and lower you down to Cyrus."

"No!" No way ever was she going to let him lower her down anywhere. "I'm coming."

She slid over the edge, pressed her feet to rocky soil, her fingers slipping in dry leaves.

"I've got you," Boone said, grabbing her waist.

"Are you sure?"

"Scout, you weigh less than my grandmother's prized turkey. Just let go!"

"Fine, but if you break your back, it's on your head." She let go, and he lowered her to the ground.

"See," he whispered in her ear, his hands still on her waist. "Piece of cake. Which, by the way, I love. If you ever happen to have a need to bake one, and you're looking for someone to eat it, I'm your man."

"I'll keep that in mind." She could have stepped away, but she liked the way it felt to be near him. Liked how secure and safe she felt when he was close. She liked the way his eyes softened when he looked at her, the way he smiled just a little, even though there really wasn't anything to smile about.

"Hate to interrupt this cozy moment," Cyrus said drily. "But I came in here to bring Scout back to the house. Jackson's orders."

If Boone was bothered by his comment, he didn't show it. "Did he bring the box?"

"With the Christmas stuff? Said it wasn't there."

"It has to be there." Scout had put the frame in it a few months after Christmas. She'd brought that and Lucy's playpen. They didn't use it anymore, but Scout hadn't had the heart to sell it. Like the frame, it had been a gift from Amber. One she'd given to Scout before the move.

"If it was, he couldn't find it."

"It should have been easy to find. I marked the box, and it was sitting right near the door."

"Maybe so, but Jackson is a pretty savvy guy. If he didn't see them, I'd guess it was because they're gone." He shrugged, his shoulders broad beneath a fitted coat. A white button-down shirt peeked out from beneath it, and his pants looked more suited for a board meeting than hostage rescue, but somehow he gave off an air of danger, his eyes so dark she couldn't see the pupils, his face hard and just a little too handsome. "He wants to bring you over there anyway. Maybe you can find the stuff. Ready?"

"Sure."

"Let's get out of here, then. I'm not an outdoorsy kind of person."

Boone snorted. "You grew up outdoors, Mitchell."

"Doesn't mean I want to grow old there. You coming back to the house or heading off to find the perp? Jackson says they've got a half dozen officers and agents combing the woods, so I'm thinking your time might be better spent somewhere else."

"You have an idea where that might be?" All the softness was gone from Boone's eyes as he glanced at Cyrus, and Scout had the distinct impression that they were exchanging an unspoken message.

"I do. I think you might be really interested, but if

you want to stay out here, suit yourself. Come on, Scout. Let's get you back home." Cyrus took her arm and started leading her away.

She didn't want to go.

Not without Boone.

Which felt strange.

She'd been just fine before he'd appeared in her life. She'd known what she needed to do, and she'd always got it done. She'd had only herself to rely on, and she'd never expected anyone to come running to the rescue.

She hadn't *needed* anyone to run to the rescue.

The fact that she needed help finding Lucy didn't change that. But she was still relieved when Boone stepped into place beside her.

They walked to the house silently, the distant sound of voices filling the quiet afternoon. Cyrus had said there were a half a dozen people searching the woods, but Scout thought there might be more. It should have comforted her to know that they were trying to track down whoever had been in the woods. All she could think about was Lucy and what her kidnapper had said. He hadn't hurt Boone, but he hadn't had the opportunity. Would he hurt Lucy?

"What are you worried about?" Boone asked as he opened the back door and ushered her inside. "Aside from the obvious."

"He said he was going to hurt Lucy if you didn't back off."

"I backed off."

"And dozens of other people went after him."

"Would you rather they waited here and did nothing?" Cyrus asked bluntly. "At least if they catch him, they might be able to get the information they need to find your daughter. They let him go and he could be gone for good. Your kid with him."

"How about you lay off a little, Mitchell? Your mean is starting to show," Boone cut in.

"I'm being honest, and I'm pretty sure Scout would rather that than a pat on the back and an 'it's going to be okay.'"

He was right, but she didn't say it. Her tea was sitting on the counter where she'd left it. Cold now, but she didn't bother heating it up. She couldn't drink it.

"Are we going to the storage unit?" she asked. It was so much easier to think about that than about Lucy being carried off to someplace where she would never be found.

"Jackson's in the living room. Why don't you go ask him?" Cyrus suggested, glancing at Boone with that same look she'd seen in the woods.

She didn't like it, and she wasn't going to ignore it. Not this time. "What's going on?"

"I already told you. We can't find the box with the Christmas stuff in it. We're going to need you to look for it." Cyrus smiled, but there was no warmth in his eyes, and Scout didn't believe a word he was saying.

"There's something else. If it has anything to do with my daughter, I want to know it."

"Scout?" Jackson appeared in the kitchen doorway. "I'm glad you're back. I've called your landlady. She's going to meet us at the storage unit to give us a hand looking for your things."

They'd planned this all out, choreographed everything, thinking that she'd just go blindly along with the plan. She wasn't going to. Not this time.

"You can meet with her yourself. I'm staying here."

She dropped down into a chair, her head aching, her pulse racing. They knew something about Lucy. She was certain of it. "Or you can tell me what's going on, and then I'll be happy to do whatever you want me to."

"You're not being reasonable," Cyrus responded. "And that's not going to help us locate your daughter."

"She's being plenty reasonable," Boone said. "And I guess if there's something that needs to be said, it may as well be said in front of her." He dropped down beside her, his thigh brushing hers, his arms crossed over his chest.

"You know the rules," Cyrus responded. "We keep things quiet until we're sure of what we're looking at."

"Sometimes rules are meant to be broken. I think this is one of those times." Boone snatched the box of animal crackers from the table, dug into it. "The way I see things, if I were in Scout's place, I'd be wanting to know every detail of the investigation."

"The way I see things," Cyrus replied, "we follow the rules, because they're there for a reason."

"You know what?" Jackson grabbed the box of animal crackers from Boone's hand. "You need to stop with the sugar, and you both need to stop bickering like a couple of old fishwives. The fact is, Scout, we got a ping on the cell phone that called yours. The police and FBI are already in the area, and we've got permission to be part of the search team."

"You think you've found her?" She jumped up, hope soaring. "I need to clean up her room, buy a new mattress for her bed."

"Hold on now." Boone grabbed her arm. "You're getting ahead of yourself. That's one of the reasons we don't usually share this kind of information. Clients get their hopes up and sometimes those hopes are dashed."

"But you may know where she is." And that was a lot. That was more than they'd had that morning.

"We've got a general area," Cyrus responded. "But we're talking miles and miles of forest. She could be anywhere in it. The best thing you can do is go with Jackson, look for the missing box. If we don't find your daughter today, that might help us find her tomorrow."

For the first time since she'd met him, he actually sounded...kind.

"He's right. For a change." Boone nudged her toward Jackson. "Go on and find the box. I'll call you if *we* find anything."

"I'd rather go with you. If you find Lucy, she's going to need me."

Boone shook his head. "That's a rule we're not going to break."

"We'd better go. Your landlady is going to be waiting." Jackson had her arm and was leading her to the door before she could think to protest.

They walked out into late-afternoon sunlight, a cold breeze scattering leaves across the driveway. In the distance, steel-gray clouds dotted the horizon. They'd have rain before sundown. Lucy loved the rain. She loved the way it pattered on the roof, and she loved jumping in puddles on the driveway.

Scout wanted to believe that her daughter would be home before the first drop fell. She wanted to believe that she'd be able to tuck Lucy into bed tonight, but she felt hollow, her faith shriveled up and useless.

Jackson opened the door of a blue SUV, and she climbed in. She thought he'd shut the door, but he stepped back and

Boone appeared, leaning in so that they were close enough for her to see the hints of green in his eyes, the tiny scar on his cheek.

"You didn't say goodbye," he said.

"No one gave me a chance."

"You know that this is the way that it has to be, right?"

She wasn't sure she did, but she was too tired to say it. Her head ached; her body ached. She wanted to go to bed and wake up and find her daughter safe in her bed.

"Scout?" He touched her cheek, his fingers warm and light against her skin. "If it could be any other way—"

"You don't have to explain."

"Yeah," he said. "I think I do. You feel helpless and hopeless, like all your power has been taken away. That's not what I want for you. What I want is for you to have your daughter back. I want you to wake up to her giggles and go to sleep knowing she's safe in her bed. I don't want you to spend the next week or month or year wondering if she's okay, wondering if she's being fed, if she's warm, if she's even alive."

Her heart jerked at the words, because she heard the pain in them, saw it on his face and in his eyes.

"I'm so sorry, Boone," she whispered, and she knew he understood, because he smiled that easy smile that was becoming as familiar as sunrise.

"So am I, but it doesn't change anything. I still wake up every morning wondering and go to bed every night wondering and live every day of my life hoping and praying that my daughter is alive. If I can keep that from happening to you, I'm going to. If that means leaving you behind while I go search, that's what I need to do."

"I understand." More than she had in the house, more than she'd have thought she could. This wasn't a power play; it wasn't Boone making decisions because he could. It was him caring deeply, wanting things to work out almost as badly as she wanted them to.

"Good, because I don't want you running off to try to find Lucy yourself. Stay with Jackson. Do what he says. I need to be fully focused on finding your daughter, and I can't waste any energy worrying that you're heading into danger."

"I won't."

"Promise me," he urged. "Because I really can't stomach the thought of you being on your own. Not after everything that's happened."

She didn't like making promises. They were difficult to keep and way too easy to break, but she couldn't deny Boone. Not when he was watching her so intently, not when he'd shared so much of his heart. "I promise," she said.

"Good." He lifted her hand, kissed her palm, folded her fingers over the spot. "I'll see you later."

He closed the door and walked away, and she sat exactly where she was, her hand fisted over his kiss, while Jackson backed out of the driveway and headed toward town.

Boone waited until the SUV disappeared from sight, then turned to face Cyrus. "Let's head out. You have the gear in your truck or do we need to try to get our hands on some?"

"Do you even need to ask?" Cyrus led the way to his Chevy Silverado.

"Would I be me if I didn't?" Boone responded as he climbed into the passenger seat of the truck.

"Would I be me if I wasn't prepared for anything?"

"I don't suppose you would be." If there was one thing Boone knew about Cyrus, the guy thought things through, planned them out. He didn't act before he knew exactly what he was going to do and how he was going to do it.

"Lucky for you. Otherwise, we'd be wasting more time trying to come up with what we need. Some of my equipment is state-of-the-art. It's not all that easy to find."

"And some of it is so old-school, they probably had it during colonial days."

"Hey, man, don't knock the old ways," Cyrus retorted, shoving a key into the ignition and starting the car. "They worked for my grandfather and great-grandfather, and they work for me."

"I wasn't knocking them. I was just pointing out that you work as well without all the fancy stuff as you do with it."

"Was that a compliment?" Cyrus asked as he pulled away from the house. "Because if it is, you must want something from me."

"Lunch would be nice." All he'd eaten in the past twenty-four hours were a few handfuls of animal crackers. If he weren't going on a search, he could have made it on that, but he was, and he knew his body enough to know what it needed to keep fueled.

"Is there ever a time when you're not thinking about your stomach, Anderson?" Cyrus grumbled, but he pulled into a fast-food parking lot and into the drive-through line.

"Generally speaking? No. Practically speaking? Yes. When we're deep in a mission, I don't think about it at all. Which is why I'd like a double cheeseburger, large fries and a soda."

Cyrus mumbled something but made the order.

Unlike Boone, he didn't eat fast food or sweets. He preferred nice meals in fancy restaurants, bottled water and lots of fruits and vegetables.

When the order was ready, he thrust the greasy bag into Boone's hands and took off again. "Happy now?"

"Ecstatic," he mumbled through a mouthful of fries. "So, how about you tell me where we're headed?"

"Twenty miles east. The signal came from somewhere around an abandoned ski resort there. The place closed down in the 1980s. Plenty of places for our perp to hide with a little girl."

"How many buildings are we talking about?"

"Fifty and a lodge spread across five thousand acres of pretty rugged terrain. The property got scooped up a couple of years ago, and the owner rents cabins during hunting season."

"Is he renting any now?"

"Six. The renters checked out. No criminal records. No connections with San Jose or the Schoepflins. At least none that Charity could find. She's still looking."

Another member of HEART, Charity was Jackson and Chance Miller's sister. Though she had specific training in search and rescue, the brothers didn't like to use her for anything more than computer research and general office help.

She wasn't happy about it, and she'd made it known.

"She's going to be upset when she hears we ran this search without her."

"She already knows, and she's already upset. I'm just hoping she doesn't show up at the search location. The

Feds are running their own K-9 team, and if she shows up with Tank, they might renege on the invitation to join the search."

"We were invited?" Boone doubted it, but he knew Chance. His boss could convince just about anyone to do anything.

"Or they were coerced." Cyrus shrugged. "Either way, we're in. I've already pinpointed the most likely location on a map. We'll check in with the local P.D. and then track in on foot. There are three cabins near a small tributary of some sort. Might be a creek or stream. Not as big as a river."

"Did you get that from Charity or look it up yourself?"

"I did a little research before I left D.C."

"You do know it's her job to provide information about locations, right?"

"She was working as fast as she could, getting me as much as she could, but up until we located the cell phone signal, her focus has been on digging into the Schoepflins' past."

"She find anything interesting?"

"Nothing that is going to help. Senator Dale Schoepflin is well liked and a shoo-in for the next election. He's been married three times. The third time seems to be the charm. He's been with Alaina Morris Schoepflin for fifteen years. No kids of her own. She pretty much raised Amber. People in their community like them. America likes them." In typical Cyrus fashion, he was spouting out facts and lots of them. The guy had a mind like a steel trap. He never forgot a detail, never missed an important piece of information.

"What about the son?"

"Christopher is even more well-known. Married to Rachel Harris. They make the rest of us look bad."

"That's it?" Boone prodded because it wasn't like Cyrus to be short on details.

"There's plenty more, but none of it is pejorative. Jackson asked Stella to head to the airport. Christopher's plane is supposed to arrive this afternoon. She's going to see if she can get a little face-to-face time with him."

"Knowing Stella, she'll manage it. Does anyone in the Schoepflin family own land out here?"

"Wouldn't that make things easy?" Cyrus asked with a cynical smile.

"What would be easy is getting to the ski resort and finding out that Lucy has already been found."

"Easy and nice," Cyrus responded. "But this is the real world, and as far as I've seen, there's not a whole lot of either of those things in it."

Boone had lived long enough to know he was right. The world was filled with things that were difficult and harsh, ugly and mean.

He'd seen the worst of the world and the people in it, but he'd also seen the best. In the midst of the darkest times, he tried to remember that.

He reached for the radio and flicked it on, filling the silence with some bluesy tune that he knew Cyrus would hate. The guy was a great team member and, most of the time, a good friend, but he didn't have much to offer in the way of positivity and optimism.

Up ahead, the road curved toward distant mountains, the afternoon sun shining gold against the fading fall foliage.

Somewhere, in the middle of that vast wilderness, Lucy was waiting to be found. He had to believe they'd find her, had to believe that God would bring them to exactly the place they needed to be at exactly the time they needed to be there in order to save her.

TWELVE

They were late, and Eleanor wasn't happy.

Scout couldn't find it in herself to care. She wanted to be with Boone, searching the woods for Lucy, not standing in a cold storage unit while her landlady shifted boxes around from one area to another.

"Are you sure it was here?" Eleanor asked, her dark eyes narrowed with irritation. "Because I don't recall seeing it when I was here last."

"I'm positive," Scout responded. "It was right next to the chair you said I could store here." She pointed to the old rocker that used to be in Lucy's room. She'd spent countless nights sitting in it, rocking her daughter to sleep. In those early days, there'd been times when she'd wanted nothing more than to fast-forward to a time when Lucy wouldn't need her so much, when getting a full night's sleep wasn't just a pipe dream.

Now Lucy almost never woke in the middle of the night. Up until the past few days, Scout had had plenty of sleep. She wanted to go back in time, though. She wanted to sit in that rocking chair in Lucy's room, inhale the sweet baby scent of shampoo and baby lotion. She wanted to enjoy every moment of looking into her daughter's face and not waste a moment wishing for something different than what was.

She blinked back tears, rubbed the knotted muscles at the back of her neck. The headache she'd had since she'd woken in the hospital was still pounding behind her eyes, but she forced herself to focus. "Someone must have moved it."

"Who?" Eleanor sighed heavily. "No one has access to the unit but my renters, and they are all upright and honest people."

"You *think* they are." Jackson lifted a tarp that had been thrown over several items. A couple of old bicycles and a jogging stroller appeared. A dresser. A lamp. A futon. No box, though.

"I did credit checks on everyone. They all pay rent on time. Never had issues with neighbors reporting loud noise or partying. No police being called to the house." She glanced at Scout. "Until recently."

"I'm really sorry about that." Scout rushed to apologize. The last thing she needed was to be kicked out of her house, and she had no doubt that Eleanor was the kind of landlord who'd be more than willing to toss someone out on the street if she thought she had a good enough reason.

"No need to apologize. I'm sure you didn't bring these troubles on yourself," Eleanor assured her, but she didn't look as if she believed it. She looked as if she was annoyed, her dark gaze scanning the storage unit, her fingers tapping a quick tattoo on her oversize leather purse.

"How many other renters use this unit?" Jackson asked. He didn't seem to be bothered by Eleanor's mood.

"Three. I already gave the FBI the list, so I don't know why we've got to go over it again." She glanced at a fancy gold watch that had probably cost more than Scout's car and frowned. "I have an appointment in thirty minutes, which means I need to leave in five. As sorry as I am for your loss, Scout—"

"She's not dead," she broke in, because she couldn't stomach Eleanor's word choice, couldn't bear to hear it.

"I meant 'lost' in a very literal sense. She is lost to you. For now. I'm sure the police and FBI will be able to track her down."

"I hope you're right." Scout pressed a hand to her stomach, trying to still its wild churning.

"They're doing everything they can to find her. These things take time and a lot of patience. I know it's hard, but you just have to keep holding on to that hope you've got. Keep cooperating. Keep working with the men and women who are searching for your daughter," Jackson said, patting her shoulder awkwardly. He meant well, but having him around wasn't anything like having Boone there. She felt cut off from the investigation, separated from the one person who'd been keeping her informed.

"I know." She didn't tell him that she was worried that no amount of work would be enough to bring her daughter home. She didn't say that she could feel every tick of the clock as the day wore on and midnight drew nearer. She didn't tell him how scared she was that when midnight came and went, her daughter really would be lost to her.

She didn't say any of those things because she didn't think Jackson would understand the way Boone did. "I just want to do my part to help the investigation move forward. The box was here. If it's not here, someone took it. There must be security cameras in a storage facility like this, right?"

"I saw them on our way in," Jackson replied. "I've

already put in a call to the local police. They're trying to get hold of the owner so the security footage can be released. For now, let's take one more look around. I didn't look inside any of the boxes when I was here earlier. Maybe that's our next step." He walked to a pile of neatly stacked boxes near the far wall.

"It's not there," Eleanor said. "Those are my things. I keep them separated from my renters'. See the blue tape on the floor? Anything within that is not to be touched by anyone but me."

"Just because something isn't supposed to be touched doesn't mean it hasn't been," Jackson pointed out.

Eleanor shrugged. "If you feel the need to check in that area, go ahead, but the boxes are sealed with packing tape. Unless they look like they've been tampered with, I'd rather you not open them."

"No problem," Jackson responded, lifting a box from the top of a stack. "Was your stuff in a white box, Scout?" he asked.

"No. Brown. With the word *Christmas* written on both sides in black marker." She eyed the pile of boxes. There were a lot. More than she remembered from her last visit. But then, she hadn't been paying any attention to Eleanor's things.

The boxes were stacked three deep and four tall, all of them white and clean and clearly marked—silverware, linens, photographs.

Scout dragged an entire stack away, looked at the stack behind it. All white.

"I do have everything alphabetized," Eleanor huffed. "I'd like it to be put back that way."

"Sure thing," Jackson responded, dragging more boxes out of the way.

And there it was, the brown box, *Christmas* emblazoned on the side.

Scout's pulse jumped, and she lifted it from the spot. "This is it."

It felt heavier than she remembered, and she set it down, lifted the lid, her breath catching as she saw the glittery Christmas balls and strands of lights. Lucy had been too young to understand the meaning of Christmas, but she'd loved the decorations. Last year, she'd been fascinated by the tree, the lights, the tiny nativity that Scout put on the coffee table.

"See anything?" Jackson asked, his words pulling her back to the moment and the task. She needed to concentrate, because the key to Lucy's disappearance could be right in front of her.

"It should be on the top. That's where I left it." She frowned, lifting several strands of lights and boxes of glass Christmas balls.

"It probably got shifted when the box was moved. What I'm interested in knowing is who moved it. But," Eleanor said, glancing at her watch again, "I really do need to get out of here. Would you mind taking the box with you so I can lock up?"

"No problem." Jackson lifted the box, turned away.

And Eleanor moved. Not in the quick short steps Scout was used to seeing. In a flurry of movement that didn't register until it was over. A quick shift of her hand. A wide arching motion of something that Scout couldn't quite see.

Jackson must have sensed it. He pivoted, the box falling from his hands, glass shattering as he lunged toward Eleanor.

She lunged, too, a wild look in her eyes and on her

face as she smashed something into his stomach, then hit him in the head with her purse.

He went down hard, his body crashing onto the concrete floor.

Scout reacted a second too late, barreling into Eleanor with enough force to send them both flying. They landed with a thud, and Scout was up again, running toward the door, escape just seconds away.

But could she leave Jackson?

What would happen if she did?

Would he be killed?

She couldn't live with that, and she stopped just outside the unit, rain pouring down on her head and soaking into her clothes.

"You can run," Eleanor said, already on her feet, the wild look gone from her eyes. "That's your choice, but I have instructions to bring you and whatever your friend sent you with me to the cabin where your daughter is being held. If you don't show up, you may never see Lucy again."

"Jackson—" She looked past Eleanor, thought she saw Jackson's hand move.

"He's fine. I didn't use enough juice to do more than knock him down for a few minutes. The brick in my purse was my employer's idea. It worked a little better than I thought it would, but I doubt he'll have more than a headache from it." She tucked a Taser in her purse, brushing a hand down her black slacks. "We leave here together, and he'll be up and moving before we pull out of the parking lot. So, how about you grab that box and everything in it, and we get going? Your daughter has been crying for you nonstop since they took her. Seems to me you'd want to get to her quick."

"Why did you take her?" Scout righted the box and started tossing things inside. Broken Christmas balls stabbed her hands, but she didn't care. "What do you want from me?"

"*I* didn't take her, and I don't want anything from you. I've seen your financial information, remember?" she said with a cold smile. "You're not worth much. Besides, I've got nothing against you. It's my employer who wants what you have. I don't know what it is, and I don't care."

"Then why are you doing this?" She lifted the last strand of lights, realized that Jackson had shifted subtly.

Was he conscious?

"Because I was offered a boatload of cash and a ticket out of the country. After today, I'm going to be living the high life in a country where the American dollar is worth a lot more than it is here. Come on." She gestured impatiently. "If I don't have you there by four, I'm out of luck and you might be, too."

"Where are we going?"

"Enough chitchat!" Eleanor barked. "You want to see your kid again?"

"Yes."

"Then let's go." She took a step, and Jackson was up, moving so quickly Scout wondered if he'd ever actually been unconscious.

One fast surge of muscle and strength, and Eleanor was facedown on the ground, her arm hiked up behind her back.

"Good job, Scout," he said, not even breathless from the effort.

"Doing what?"

"Getting a little more information than we had before." He dragged Eleanor to her feet. "Now, how about we all head out together? Because I really hate to be left out of the party."

"You're going to have to figure out where we're going first," Eleanor spat. "And I'm not telling you. I do that and I may as well shoot myself in the head right now."

"Let's not be dramatic, Eleanor," Jackson said drily. "You're here, you're safe, and as long as you cooperate, I'm going to make sure you stay that way. We're going to take your car. I hope you don't mind."

"I do," she growled, tugging against his hold.

"Too bad. I wouldn't want your boss to realize your mission wasn't successful. I'm sure he's got someone watching the facility to make sure your car leaves with you in it. Scout, want to get her keys out of her purse?"

Scout picked up Eleanor's oversize bag, pulled out the brick and dropped it onto the ground. Found a wallet, a cell phone, the Taser and, finally, the keys.

"Got them," she said, her voice shakier than she wanted it to be.

"Good." Jackson took them from her hand. "So, here's how it's going to be, Eleanor. You get to drive, and you'd better drive well, because the amount of time you spend in jail is going to depend on it."

"You're assuming that there's going to be jail time."

He laughed. "Come on, lady. You hit me over the head with a brick. You zapped me with a Taser. There are two witnesses who heard you confess to being paid by a little girl's kidnapper. You're in deep. You cooperate and you can dig yourself out a little."

Eleanor pressed her lips together, but didn't respond.

"I'll take your silence for assent. Let's go. Scout, if

you can manage the box, we'll be set." He dragged Eleanor outside, and Scout followed with the box.

The day had grown darker, rain pouring from the sky in sheets.

If the temperature dropped, there would be ice in the mountains. Would they call off the search for Lucy if that happened?

Jackson opened the trunk, had Scout put the box in it and then urged her into the passenger seat. As soon as she was in, he walked Eleanor to the driver's side of the car. "I'm riding in the back. I've got a feeling Eleanor's boss has someone stationed outside the storage facility and I don't want to be seen driving this car. Play nice," he ordered as he opened the driver's-side door. "I've got a headache, and I'm not going to be happy if you don't."

He climbed in the backseat, then handed Eleanor the keys.

She shoved one of them in the ignition and started the engine, her jaw tight, her gaze focused straight ahead. "Where do you want me to take you?"

"Same place you were going before I decided not to cooperate with your plans," Jackson responded.

"I'm not going to do it."

"Then just drive yourself to jail, because that's where you're headed."

"I'll be out on bond before you can sign your name on the complaint."

"How much do you think that's going to be for someone who's been arrested for kidnapping, attempted murder—?"

"I wasn't trying to kill you!" Eleanor protested.

"I'm not talking about me. I'm talking about Scout."

"I had nothing to do with what happened to her."

"But you knew she was going to be attacked, and you did nothing about it."

"I didn't! All I knew was that Lucy was going to be held as collateral. No one was supposed to get hurt."

"Held as collateral?" Jackson snorted. "That's a pretty way of saying she was being held for ransom. Kidnapping is kidnapping. No matter the name you put on it. Murder is murder, too."

"No one was murdered," she snapped.

"What do you think is going to happen to Lucy when your boss realizes you weren't successful? You think he's going to try to run with her?" Jackson said, his words like knives to Scout's heart. "If so, you're a fool."

Eleanor didn't speak. Not a word as she drove down Main Street and made her way through River Valley.

Scout wanted to fill the silence. She wanted to beg for the information, demand it, offer anything to have it.

She knew it wouldn't do any good. Eleanor had never been warm or friendly. She'd never been unkind, either. All Scout could do was pray that she'd be reasonable, that in the deepest part of whoever she was, she'd understand the value of Lucy's life and agree to do what it would take to save it.

Finally, Eleanor sighed. "I'll take you there, but only for the kid's sake. She's a sweet little thing, and I don't want anything to happen to her."

"Thank you," Scout breathed, and Eleanor scowled.

"I already said that this is for Lucy. Not for you. Now, how about both of you just shut up and let me drive. Otherwise, I might change my mind."

"I have to make a few phone calls," Jackson replied. "But I'll try to keep the talking to a minimum."

Scout wanted to ask if he was calling Boone, but she was so afraid that she'd annoy Eleanor, she kept her mouth shut as River Valley disappeared behind them and the mountains loomed ever closer up ahead.

THIRTEEN

Boone's phone rang as he and Cyrus geared up.

He answered quickly, his mind on the mission ahead. "Anderson here. What's up?"

"I'm heading in your direction with Scout and her landlady," Jackson responded.

"I'm assuming you have a good reason for that?" Boone shrugged into his pack and slipped a parka on over it. The temperature was going to drop as the sun went down, and he needed to stay as dry as possible.

"Eleanor was planning to take Scout to visit her daughter. She thought she'd do it without me, but things didn't work out that way."

Boone stilled, rain pouring down around him, Cyrus mumbling something about getting a move on because the sun set early in November. "She knows where Lucy is?"

Cyrus looked up from the GPS he was programming. "Who knows?" he asked.

Boone raised a hand, silencing him as he tried to hear above the pounding rain.

"Says she was paid to take care of the kid while her boss looked for whatever it is he thinks Scout has," Jackson said.

"Who's her boss?"

"Who is *she?*" Cyrus moved closer, his dark eyes flashing with impatience. A hundred yards behind him, a three-story building jutted up against low-hanging clouds, the windows and doors boarded up, graffiti marring the dingy white facade. The place had probably been beautiful at its peak. Now the neglected lodge was nothing but an eyesore in the midst of stunning wilderness.

"She says she doesn't know." Jackson answered Boone's question. "He contacted her a month ago, asking questions about Scout and Lucy. Offered her a few thousand dollars to snoop around the house."

"I was *not* snooping," a woman called. "It's my property. It is within my legal right to inspect it."

"Save it for the police," Jackson growled.

"I take it that's Eleanor? Did she say how she got involved in all this?"

"Long story short, the guy who hired her to *inspect* Scout's things asked if she'd like to earn a nice chunk of change and a plane ticket out of the country. All she had to do for it was babysit Lucy for a few days while he found the thing he was looking for."

"She have any idea what that thing is?"

"Not that she's admitting to. We've got the box with the picture frame in it. Haven't found the frame yet, though. We got a little sidetracked. The good news is, Eleanor has the exact coordinates of the cabin where they're keeping Lucy. It's a tough three-mile hike through the woods, but we shouldn't have any trouble finding it."

"Go ahead and give me the location. I'll—"

"I don't think so, Boone. We're going to have to think

this through. We go in there half-cocked and someone is liable to get hurt."

"Since when do I do things half-cocked?"

"Since the day I met you."

Boone couldn't argue with that.

He did go with his gut a lot, move into situations on a hunch. He never did it without knowing exactly what he was getting into, though. He didn't this time. He had no idea if there was one person or ten or none at the cabin with Lucy.

"Okay. Fine. What's the plan?" he asked, glancing over his shoulder at the police and FBI agents who were gathered beneath a canvas awning in the ski resort's parking lot. They'd already drawn a grid of the area, divided it into quadrants. Search dogs were sniffing at the ground, but no one had moved into the woods yet. No one would until the perimeter of the area had been secured. That required man power and coordination from local police in two counties. Those things took time. Which was one of the reasons Boone preferred to work outside of local law-enforcement channels.

"We're almost there. Hold off until we arrive. I already put in calls to Rodriguez and Lamar. They've given me permission to send Scout and Eleanor in ahead of the search teams."

"No." He said it definitively, because there was no way he was letting it happen. Scout was too fragile, too wounded. Sending her out into the wilderness with a woman who'd already admitted to working with Lucy's kidnapper was a surefire way to get her killed.

"That's not your decision to make," Jackson responded.

"It's not yours, either."

"Right. It's Scout's, and she's already decided."

"Probably because she doesn't know what she's getting into."

"She knows. I explained everything."

"I think I should explain it again."

"We're pulling into the parking area now," Jackson responded. "Knock yourself out."

Boone glanced at the entrance to the parking lot, saw a dark sedan rolling in. It pulled up beside Cyrus's truck, the front passenger's door opening almost before it came to a full stop.

Scout climbed out, her skin pallid, the staples a dark stain against the paleness. Her hair hung around her shoulders, the strands tangled and matted from rain. She shouldn't have been beautiful, but she met his eyes and smiled, and there was absolutely nothing about her that wasn't lovely.

He took her hand, pulled her away from Cyrus, the truck, the sedan. "You okay?" he asked, and she nodded.

"I'm not the one who's been standing out in the rain, so I guess I'm fine." She swiped her hand across his cheek and frowned. "You, on the other hand, are soaked."

"Not even close, but *you* will be if you head out into those woods. You don't have the gear for it. No parka. No hiking boots. You'll be frozen before you get a hundred yards in."

"Do you really think I care?" She glanced at the building that had once served as the ski resort's lodge, eyed the forest that stretched out beyond it. "I would walk a thousand miles in the snow to get to my daughter, and I know you would do the same for yours. Don't make this be about discomfort or hardship. All it's about is love. I have enough of that to get me through anything."

There were a lot of things he could have said. He

could have told her how dangerous it might be. He could have said that she might get to the location and find that Lucy had already been moved. He could have told her the harsh truth of the matter—that love wasn't always enough. He could have formulated a dozen arguments against her going with Eleanor, but she was right. He'd have walked over burning coals to get to Kendal. "Tell you what," he said. "I won't make it about anything but doing everything I can to help you."

She smiled at that. "Thanks, Boone. When this is all over, I'm going to make you that cake you want."

"Is that a promise? Because I take promises about food very seriously."

"It's a promise."

"Are we talking chocolate? Yellow? Angel food?"

"We're talking whatever you like best."

"What I like best," he said quietly, "are blond-haired librarians with staples in their foreheads."

That surprised a laugh out of her. "Thank you. I think."

"You two done over there?" Jackson called, his tone just shy of being amused. "Because we've got some planning to do before the ladies head to the cabin. They don't get there by five and our guy might get suspicious."

"Four," a dour-looking woman with dark hair and pale green eyes said. Eleanor Finch. He'd seen her at Scout's house, but he hadn't thought much of it because she'd had plenty of reason to be there. "He was very specific about that. If I'm not there by then, he's not going to wait around."

"Okay, then," Jackson responded. "We have even less time, and we have a lot to talk through. How about we get under the tarp and hash things out with the rest of the team?"

"How about we pretend we did and just come up with our own plan?" Cyrus responded.

"Great idea except for two things," Jackson said, rubbing at a lump on the side of his forehead. It was blue and red with a few hints of green and yellow mixed in. Obviously, he'd left a few things out during their phone conversation. "First, I'm not in the frame of mind that's required to irritate the local police and the FBI all at one time. Second, I'm not in the mood to irritate my brother."

"Your brother is always irritated," Boone pointed out. He liked Chance Miller, enjoyed working for him, had even gone on a couple of hunting trips with the guy. But facts were facts, and the fact was, Chance spent a good portion of his life trying to micromanage the world. It made for a well-run, successful business, but it didn't do much for the happiness quotient.

"Yeah, well, seeing as how I got beaned on the head with a brick today, I'm not feeling all that happy, either. So, how about we follow the rules on this? We've got a two-year-old child to think about. The more heads we put together to plan the rescue, the better."

"Then let's get to planning."

"I'd prefer we not stand out in the rain to do it," Eleanor grumbled.

"Not that I care all that much what you prefer," Jackson said, "but there's probably room for us under the tarp. Rodriguez and Lamar should be here soon, and we can get this show on the road."

"I'd like to get it on the road now," Scout murmured, but she didn't protest when Boone pressed a hand to her lower back and urged her across the parking lot. She stayed close as Rodriguez and Lamar arrived, hovering near his elbow as the team formulated a plan, went over every detail again and again and again. He could sense her impatience to get moving, but she didn't voice it, didn't try to rush the process.

That impressed him.

She impressed him.

Rather than panic, she focused, and that was going to serve them all well in the next few hours. If they'd been alone, he would have told her that, but they were surrounded by a dozen agents and officers.

"That's it," Special Agent Rodriguez said, her dark gaze settling on Scout. "Are you sure you're up to this? If you don't think you can do it, we'll have an agent step in for you."

"I don't think any of your agents are going to be able to pass for me," Scout responded.

"We can find someone," Rodriguez assured her, but Scout shook her head.

"I'll be fine."

Rodriguez eyed her for a moment and nodded. "Just make sure you do exactly what we've discussed. Don't veer from the plan. If you do, things could go bad really quickly."

"I won't," Scout assured her.

Boone wondered if she meant it. She probably *thought* she meant it.

The problem was, when it came to love, the heart worked a lot faster than the head.

"Do we have the frame Amber sent you?" Officer Lamar asked, and Scout shook her head.

"I haven't had a chance to look for it yet."

"You have the box?"

"In Eleanor's car."

"Let's get it. If you're going to pull this off, you need to have something to bargain with."

If.

Scout didn't much like the word.

There was too much room in it for error, too much of a chance that the thing she didn't want would come true. Everything had been explained to her in excruciating detail. Every word she needed to say, every move she needed to make. *If* she did those things, she might get her daughter back. But she might not, and that was the thing that was killing her.

She followed Officer Lamar to Eleanor's car, waiting while Jackson opened the trunk. She felt sick, her head pounding, the cold wind spearing through her coat. Boone had been right about her not being prepared for the weather. She'd been standing outside for an hour, and she felt cold to the bone.

"There it is," Jackson said, pointing at the box. The contents were a jumbled mess, strands of lights and shards of colored glass mixed up together.

"Is the frame in there?" Boone leaned over Scout's shoulder, his breath ruffling her hair, his warmth seeping through her coat and chasing away some of the chill.

"I don't know. We didn't get a chance to look." She shoved some of the lights aside, lifting out boxes of broken glass balls. The frame had been on the top of the pile before, but if Eleanor had gone through the box, it could be at the bottom.

"It's in there," Eleanor said.

"And you know this how?" Officer Lamar asked.

"Here's the deal," Eleanor huffed. "I'm cold. I'm wet. And I'm already in more trouble than I want to be. I want to get this over with sooner rather than later. So, I'm just tossing the information out there. I went through the box a couple of weeks ago. I was told to look for journals or letters. There weren't any in there, but I did see a picture frame."

Scout plunged in deeper, nearly falling over in her effort to get to the bottom of the box.

"Careful," Boone murmured, his hands settling on her waist. He left them there as she pushed aside several ornaments, spotted something pink and glittery near the bottom of the box.

"Here!" She pulled it out, the picture a colored photo that must have been taken during one of her first play-dates with Amber. They'd been young. Maybe eight or nine years old, their hair in pigtails. Even then, Amber had been a rebel, the ends of her ponytails died purple with grape juice. If Scout remembered correctly, Amber's parents hadn't been happy about it.

"Glitzy," Boone said, touching the edge of the frame.

"That's how Amber was. She liked showy things, glittery things. The more it sparkled, the happier she was." She smiled at the memory.

"Much as I'm enjoying your trip down memory lane," Eleanor griped, "I'd like to get this over with. The hike is difficult on the best of days. It's going to be atrocious today."

"Mind if I take a look at that?" Special Agent Rodriguez asked, ignoring Eleanor's comment.

Scout handed it to her reluctantly, waited impatiently as she studied the photo and then flipped over the frame.

"Ever opened it?" she asked.

"No. I never had a reason to. Amber wrote me a note saying I should switch out the photo and put one of me and Lucy in there, but I loved the one she put in it, so I didn't bother."

"She said you should or could?" Boone asked, his brow furrowed.

"Should. She mentioned it three or four times in the Christmas card that came with it."

"Mind if I open the back?" Special Agent Rodriguez asked, her fingers already working at the tiny clasp on the back. She opened it up. Scout didn't know what she expected, but there was nothing there but the photo, a few numbers and letters scrawled on the back. "This mean anything to you?" She handed the photo to Scout.

Don't forget to visit.
J.A.C. 6/02/97
M.E.C. 11/15/04

"I don't…" *…think so* was what she was going to say, but then it hit her like a ton of bricks. The letters. The numbers. "My parents," she said, so surprised the picture almost fell from her hands.

Boone took it, eyeing it as if it had more secrets to reveal. "Those are their initials?"

"And the day each of them died. Amber was at both of their funerals. It was just the three of us in my family. No uncles or aunts or grandparents. She stood in as family."

"She says you shouldn't forget to visit," he pointed out. "Is she speaking about their grave sites?"

"Probably. They were buried in the family crypt in San Jose. Once a month, Amber and I would place flowers there. When I left San Jose, she promised to continue doing it."

"Interesting," Special Agent Rodriguez said. "I think

I'll send an agent out to check out the grave sites. Can you give me an address?"

She did as she was asked, feeling almost as if Amber were there, trying to convey some secret message. If only she knew what that message was. "I wish I'd seen that sooner. Maybe…"

"What?" Boone asked, handing the photo back to her.

"Maybe it was a cry for help. Maybe she was telling me that I shouldn't forget to visit her grave site after she died."

"I doubt such a flamboyant person would send such a subtle message," Boone said. "Based on what I've read and what you've told me, I'd say that if Amber knew she was going to die, she'd have been more likely to send you a bouquet of balloons with her epitaph written on them than a cryptic message."

"You're probably right. Amber always did things in a big way." Scout's heart ached as she thought about her friend and the message she'd tried to send. Had she expected Scout to find it before she'd died?

"It's possible there is more to the message. She might have left something at the grave site. My people will check things out in San Jose," Special Agent Rodriguez cut in. "For now, though, we need to focus on Lucy. Let's put the photo back in the frame and get moving."

Scout would have been happy to do it, but her hands were shaking from cold or, maybe, from nerves. No matter how many times she told herself and everyone else that she was prepared to go after Lucy, she wasn't sure it was true.

She was terrified that she'd forget what she'd been told, walk into a situation that was nothing like what she was expecting and somehow do something that would cause Lucy to be hurt—or worse. She *wanted* to make the long trek through the forest and come out an hour or two later with her daughter. She just wasn't sure she had it in her. She'd spent her entire life playing it safe. The one night she'd done something different, gone out of her comfort zone, played the game by different rules, she'd ended up pregnant and alone, starting her life all over again in a town far away from everything she'd ever known.

That hadn't proved anything about her adventurous spirit or her ability to buck the system and play by her own rules. All it had done was prove that she had the ability to make a stupid decision, disappoint herself and disappoint God.

"Let me," Boone said, brushing her hands away from the frame and sliding the photo back in. "There you go."

"Thanks," she said, tucking the frame into her coat pocket, her fingers and nose cold, her heart a leaden weight in her chest. She felt sick, her head aching, her stomach churning. She didn't know how much of that was from her head wound and how much was from nerves, but she really hoped she wouldn't lose her breakfast in front of a dozen law-enforcement officials.

"You don't have to do this, Scout. There are other options." He cupped her cheek, looked into her eyes. For a moment it was just the two of them, standing in the rain, a thousand promises dancing in the air between them, a thousand dreams just out of reach. She wanted to step into his arms, rest her aching head against his chest, but they weren't alone, and her daughter was waiting in a cabin just a few miles away.

"None of them are as good," she said, because it was true. They'd discussed every option during the hour-long planning session. None of them made as much sense as the one she'd agreed to—she and Eleanor walking to the cabin escorted by Boone until they were a quarter mile away. The remainder of the team spreading out in the woods, surrounding the cabin before Scout and Eleanor arrived. Everyone moving silently and stealthily, giving Lucy's kidnapper no indication that they were there. If everything went as planned, Scout and Eleanor would be allowed to leave with Lucy once the frame was delivered.

Barring that, Scout would take Lucy into one of the cabin bedrooms, signal by opening a window that they were away from the kidnapper and wait for their rescue.

Everyone involved in the planning had admitted that it wasn't a perfect plan, but it was their best option for a good outcome for Lucy.

That was all Scout cared about.

"No," Boone admitted, his hand dropping to her nape, his fingers warm and a little rough against her skin. "But there are good-enough options."

"Would good enough work for you if this were Kendal?"

His eyes darkened, and he shook his head. "No, and that's the only reason why I'm not fighting tooth and nail against this plan."

"You could fight it with more than that and it would still be what it is," Cyrus cut in, impatience in his voice and on his face. He didn't look like the kind of guy who liked to wait around, and he'd been pacing the edges of the group almost from the moment the planning had begun. "So, how about we get going? Four o'clock will be here soon, and if Lucy is moved, we're going to have to spend a long night hunting these woods for her."

The thought was enough to get Scout going.

She moved away from Boone, shrugging into a black parka someone offered, the vinyl-like material doing nothing to warm her chilled skin. Her feet were soaked through her tennis shoes, her jeans clinging to her legs.

It didn't matter.

Nothing did.

Except finding Lucy and bringing her home.

FOURTEEN

The storm whipped itself into a wild frenzy as Boone led Scout and Eleanor into the woods. Marked paths had once shown the way from the lodge to the rental cabins and ski areas. Time and neglect had hidden them. Aside from a few painted arrows on tree trunks, there was no indication that large groups of people had once vacationed in the area.

"Which way?" he asked Eleanor. He had the coordinates she'd provided, and his GPS was pointing the way. He wanted to test her, though. See how helpful she planned to be.

"South. Just keep heading in that direction until we hit the creek. Then we turn east. It's about a half mile from there. It usually takes me a little over an hour. It's going to take longer today." She pulled her hood up over her hair, buttoned her coat. She'd worn thin-looking black slacks and black hiking boots. She'd have been better off in jeans. She'd been offered a parka and refused, claiming that her boss would get suspicious if she and Scout showed up wearing the same thing.

She had a point.

She also had more explaining to do. No one believed

her claim that she didn't know the man who had hired her. He was someone within her sphere of influence, and that relationship had led to her involvement. Eventually, the truth would come out. For now, he'd pretend he believed every word Eleanor said if that meant accomplishing the goal and completing the mission.

The wind picked up, the rain mixing with sleet as they climbed a steep hill and headed down the other side. Already, they were cut off from civilization, the view of the lodge hidden by the slope they were descending.

Scout slipped, and he caught her arm just in time to keep her from sliding down the last hundred yards of the slope.

"Careful," he said, keeping his hand on her elbow as they picked their way down the last several yards. "You break an ankle and we're in trouble."

"I'm sure if that happened, your friends would find a solution to the problem," Eleanor muttered, holding on to sapling trees as she made her way down ahead of them. "Must be nice to have so many people fighting for you. Me? I've got no one. My no-good husband dumped me the day I turned forty. Left me with a mortgage and a debt that I didn't think I was ever going to pay off. No kids. Thank goodness! The last thing I need are a few of his brats trying to spend every bit of the money I've managed to scrape together over the past ten years."

"She's just a little bitter," Scout whispered, slipping again, her fingers grasping on to his shirt as she tried to maintain her balance. "And I am really regretting my decision to wear tennis shoes this morning."

"There isn't enough tread in the world to keep someone from slipping on this stuff," he responded, keeping his gaze on Eleanor. She was increasing her pace, and he had a feeling she was going to make a break for it.

Maybe she thought she could get to the cabin, convince her boss to give her the plane ticket and money she really seemed to believe he had for her, before the dragnet they'd created closed in.

It wasn't going to happen.

Boone didn't bother telling her that.

She wouldn't have believed it.

He kept an eye on her progress as he helped Scout over a fallen log. "Looks like your landlady is trying to ditch us."

"You can run up ahead and stop her, if you want. I'll catch up as quickly as I can."

"There's no point. She gets too far ahead and someone will grab her and hold her for us."

"What if they don't?" she asked, picking up her pace so that she was nearly jogging.

"Do you really think they're going to let her get to the cabin before you?" He ducked under a low-hanging pine bough, tugging her under behind him.

"I don't know anything anymore, Boone," she replied, her words so quiet he could barely hear them over the storm. "One day, everything was great. I had a job and a daughter and a life that was exactly what I wanted. The next, everything was ripped away from me, and now…"

"What?"

"I just want Lucy home. Then I can figure out the rest of it."

"Like what we're going to be when this is over?" he asked, tracking Eleanor as she trudged up another hill.

"We? As in us?" Scout asked, and he didn't think she was surprised by the thought, didn't think she hadn't thought about it before. There was something between them, a connection that had been building since the moment he'd seen her in the grocery store. Where that would lead, what it would bring them to, was something that he was ready and willing to explore.

"Why not? We're both single and unattached," he responded. Life was too short to beat around the bush.

"I'm not unattached. I have Lucy."

"There are plenty of people in relationships who have a child or two," he pointed out, and she frowned, rainwater and ice sliding off her parka hood and dripping onto her cheeks.

"I know, but if I get Lucy back, I can go back to what I had before she was taken. My job, my church family, my friends. Every day just kind of the same as the one before. That's the way I like it, Boone."

"Safe?"

"Yes."

"That's a problem for us, then. It's never going to be safe if I'm in your life. There's always going to be the risk that I won't come back from a mission, that the next time I get on a plane will be the last time you see me."

"I know."

"So, maybe the two of us together isn't such a good thing." He offered her an easy out, because he didn't want her to live with regrets, didn't want her heart broken the way his had been when Lana walked away.

"Maybe it's not," she responded, and there was so much sadness in her voice, he wanted to pull her into his arms, tell her that sometimes the reward outweighed the risk.

There wasn't time.

Eleanor crested the rise, paused at the top, turning to look back at them and waving impatiently.

"I guess she decided not to leave us," Scout said, sprinting forward as if the most important thing in the world was catching up to her landlady.

He'd scared her with talk of a future together. He knew it.

He didn't regret his words, though.

Life was finite. In a fraction of a second it could end. A bullet, an explosion, a knife attack. Or the more mundane: car accident, heart attack, falling tree. He glanced at the heavy-laden spruce trees that were bowing with the force of the wind. He was always on guard, always watching, and that made him more than a little aware of just how little time there was. He never wanted to waste any of it, never wanted to miss an opportunity to go where God was leading.

If He was leading to Scout, if He had brought Boone there, that was where Boone wanted to stay. No matter the risk. No matter the potential for heartache.

All he needed to know was that Scout wanted to be there, too.

The thought was better left for another time, though.

Time was ticking away, the afternoon wearing on, the sun already sinking behind dark clouds. Darkness came early in the mountains. Even without the four o'clock deadline that Eleanor had been given, they'd have had to hurry. Already, the woods were shrouded with shadows, the icy rain and wind limiting visibility. Things were only going to get worse as the day wore on, and every bit of Boone's focus had to be on getting to the cabin and getting Lucy out.

He caught up with Scout easily, taking her arm as she

trudged the last few steps to Eleanor. She didn't meet his eyes, refused to glance his way, and he thought that maybe the moisture sliding down her cheeks wasn't just icy rain. Maybe there were tears mixed in, as well.

"It's about time," Eleanor snapped. "Do you know what time it is? We'll never make it to the cabin at the rate we're going."

"We'll make it," Boone assured her.

"It was all that planning," she continued as if he hadn't spoken. "A huge waste of valuable time. For all any of us knows, Gaige decided to go back to leave with the kid and without me. He cleaned out the San Jose bank accounts, so he's got plenty of money to do it. He and Lucy could be miles away by now, while we try to execute some stupid plan come up with by a bunch of nincompoop federal agents and foolhardy local—"

"What do you mean *cleaned out the bank accounts in San Jose?*" He cut her off midtirade. "I thought you said you didn't know anything about the guy."

"I don't."

"Then how do you know he has bank accounts in San Jose?"

"He must have mentioned it to me when we were making arrangements for payments," she responded, her face suddenly devoid of color. She was afraid. That was something she hadn't shown before, and that made Boone a lot more nervous than he'd already been.

"I don't think so," Boone said. "I think you know him well. I think you've probably known him for years."

"And I think you're full of it," she scoffed, but the fear was still there, her dark eyes hollow.

"You're scared of him, aren't you?" he asked, and she

pressed her lips together, trudging on as if she hadn't heard him.

"What? Is he a boyfriend? Some guy who abuses you?" He offered her an explanation, curious to see if she latched on to it.

"Of course not! Gaige would never lay a hand on me. Not in that way! He's…a friend. Someone I met a couple of years ago."

"You're in a relationship with him," Boone said. He didn't make it a question, because he already knew the answer, had heard the same sorry story play out too many times to count. "And he already has a wife and a couple of kids, right?"

"It's none of your business," she snapped.

"Which means he does. Have you met her?"

"Who?"

"The wife? The one he's left behind so that he can run off with you? How about the kids? How many does he have? Two? Three? Is he missing their ball games and school plays to spend time with you?" He poked at her, hoping to get her riled up enough to let a little more information slip.

"His kids are grown, and his wife is cold as a dead fish. He says—"

"I'm sure he says a lot." He cut her off. Not really interested in the details. "Did he promise to leave them if you helped him with this? Did he say you two would run off together once he got what he wanted?"

"You know nothing about anything!"

"I know plenty. I've seen this over and over again. Do you know how many women I've met who are just like you? So desperate, they'll believe any lie to have the thing they think they need."

"I'm not desperate, and the only thing I need is for you to shut up!" she shouted, her eyes blazing, her hands fisted.

"And I need you to realize you're being used. Once you do, then you can be useful to yourself and to us."

"I'm not interested in being useful to you, and I'm *not* being used."

"Right," Boone said, snorting for good measure.

"It's true! He showed me the tickets and the passports last night. Everything is set. As soon as I get to the cabin, we're supposed to leave for the airport. He decided we shouldn't fly out of any nearby airports, so he's got us booked on a flight leaving from New York. He laid the whole itinerary out for me last night. First New York, then L.A. After that—" She stopped short of finishing, but it was too late. She'd already said more than she'd intended.

He knew it.

She knew it.

"You really think that's what was going to happen?" Boone said, wanting to push her even harder, make her even angrier, keep her talking about Gaige's plans. "I've been doing my job for a long time, Eleanor, and I can tell you for sure that if he'd wanted to run off with you, he'd have been waiting for you outside that storage unit. You'd have gone to the airport from there, climbed on board a plane and been at some romantic getaway before the sun rose tomorrow morning."

"He didn't want to be seen."

"I don't see why not. We don't know who he is. We don't know what he looks like. He could be standing five feet from me, and I wouldn't know it."

"He couldn't leave Lucy alone, and if he'd taken her with him, someone might have recognized her."

"He's good—I'll give him that. The argument would almost be convincing if I didn't know he has accomplices. Aside from you, there have to be at least three or four people working with him. I saw them following Scout the night Lucy was kidnapped. One of them could have stayed with Lucy while you two took off."

"They're gone. He paid them and sent them away, because he was afraid too many strangers in such a small town would draw people's attention. He's smart that way." She turned away, started walking again, picking her way over fallen logs and through ankle-deep puddles. She was obviously finished with the conversation. That was fine. He could let it go. He'd got more information than he'd thought he would.

Apparently Scout didn't feel the same.

"Did you see the tickets?" she asked, her breath panting out, hot and raspy. She looked worn-out and ready to collapse, but he knew she'd keep going until she found her daughter. That was another thing he'd seen too many times to count. There was no limit to a parent's love, no way to measure just how far someone would go, how hard she'd push herself for the sake of her child.

"Of course I did," Eleanor huffed. "All three of them."

She must not have realized what she'd said, but Scout did. She grabbed her arm, pulled her to a stop. "How many tickets did he have, Eleanor?"

Eleanor stood silently for so long Boone wondered if she'd answer.

Finally, she looked straight at Scout. There was no color in her face, no emotion. The words, when they came, were as dead as her expression. "Three. One was for Lucy. He said we'd be a family. The three of us."

"You were planning to take her out of the country and never come back?" Scout sounded horrified, her eyes wide with shock.

"We were going to give her what you couldn't."

"There is nothing that she needs that I can't give," Scout replied, her voice pulsing with all the emotions that were absent from Eleanor.

"You're too young to realize how limited your life is, how little you really have to offer Lucy."

"That is one of the most insulting things anyone has ever said to me!" Scout protested, but Eleanor started walking again, stepping over a fallen tree and ducking under a low-hanging branch.

"I didn't mean it as an insult. You're a nice young woman. You work hard. You pay your bills on time. But there are plenty of things that you can't provide your daughter—culture, wealth, an opportunity to be something more than a small-town kid living a small-town life."

"I think she'd rather have her mother than those things," Boone cut in, and Eleanor sent a hard look in his direction.

"Lucy isn't even three yet. Her mother is whoever happens to be taking care of her."

"That's not true!" Scout sputtered.

"Maybe not, but in a few months, she'd have almost forgotten you. In a year, you wouldn't even be a memory. Same for you. Eventually, you'd have had other children and forgotten all about Lucy."

"I would never ever have forgotten Lucy." Scout bit out every word, the weight of them hanging in the air.

"Like I said, you're young," Eleanor replied blithely. "You have no idea how fleeting and fragile love is. You have it one minute. The next it's gone and you move on to someone else."

Something inside Scout must have snapped.

She lunged forward, rage seeping from every pore, pulsing from every muscle.

Boone just managed to grab her before she made contact, pulling her up short and wrapping both arms around her waist.

"Cool it," he said quietly. "She's not worth your anger."

"I am not angry. I'm infuriated!" She shoved at his arms. "How dare she say that I would forget my daughter!"

"I meant it in a benign way," Eleanor tried to explain, but Scout wasn't having any of it.

She wiggled out of Boone's grip and pointed her finger in Eleanor's face. "You are nuts if you think that anything you just said to me was benign!"

"She's nuts," Boone cut in, pulling Scout back into his arms, because he wasn't sure he could trust her to *not* tear into Eleanor, "if she thinks Gaige was actually going to take her on that plane. I'd venture a guess that the passport and ticket weren't for her. Did you get a look at the photo in the passport, Eleanor? Did he give you a good close look at it?"

She lifted her chin. "I didn't have to. I trust him."

"Trust in men is often unfounded," Boone responded.

"Not in this case. Gaige has always been trustworthy."

"Except when it comes to his wife and kids?" Scout asked, and Eleanor frowned.

"They didn't earn his trust. I have. Not that it matters," Eleanor responded. "I won't be going anywhere. Except jail. The way I see it, if I have to be there, he may as well be, too. The problem is, if we don't get to the cabin by four, he's going to leave. His flight takes off at one tomorrow morning, and he warned me that if I didn't make it back to the cabin in time, he'd go without me. He'll do it, too. I can tell you that right now. He'll take Lucy and he'll leave the country, and no one will ever see either of them again."

She marched away, chin tilted so high Boone was surprised she didn't drown.

"Wow!" Scout breathed, sagging against Boone, her slim weight pressing against his chest and abdomen. He had a moment of pure insanity, a moment when all he could think about was how good she felt in his arms, how right it was to be standing there with her.

"Wow what?" he asked, stepping back, giving himself a little breathing room.

"Does she really believe he was going to take her to some exotic location? Did she really think that the two of them could travel with my daughter and not get noticed?"

"You said it yourself—she's crazy."

"There's crazy, and then there is *crazy*," Scout sighed. "She's both."

He nearly laughed at that, but they had a job to do, and standing around chatting about things wasn't getting it done. "At least we have some information to go on. Airport. Time. Connecting flight."

"It's great to have, but if he leaves the cabin with Lucy—"

"Don't borrow trouble, Scout." He pressed his hand to her back, urging her in the direction Eleanor had gone.

"How is it borrowing trouble to think through the possibilities?"

"It steals energy away from dealing with the realities.

Right now, the reality is that we don't know what we're going to find at the cabin. Until we get there, there's nothing we can do but keep running with plan A."

"Is there a plan B?"

"If we need one."

"Are you going to tell me what it is?"

"Once I come up with it, sure."

She laughed shakily. "You're a funny guy, Boone."

"I'm also a hungry guy, so how about we get this show on the road and bring your daughter home so you can make me that cake we were discussing?"

"You make me believe," she responded, "that those things are really going to happen."

"Believing is half the battle."

"What's the other half?" Scout asked.

"Knowing that whatever happens, God is in control of it, and that it really will be okay." He took her hand as they headed up another steep hill, Eleanor marching a few yards ahead, her shoulders slumped as if the reality of what she'd done was finally settling in.

She was smart to feel defeated. By the time they reached the cabin, it would be surrounded by law-enforcement officials. There was no way Gaige would ever make it past the blockades that were being set or the armed men and women who were lying in wait. If he tried, he'd be stopped.

FIFTEEN

Lucy's prison was nicer than Scout had imagined.

Or maybe it was the distance that was making it appear that way. From a quarter mile back, the log cabin looked to be in pristine condition, its tin roof sparkling with millions of tiny ice pellets.

Scout squinted as she looked through the binoculars Boone had handed her, focusing on the windows, trying desperately to catch some glimpse of Lucy while he texted their location to the team, made sure everyone was in place.

Eleanor stood under the canopy of an old oak, head down, a layer of ice coating her hood and coat. She hadn't spoken a word since she'd admitted that they'd planned to leave the country with Lucy.

Was she regretting the confession?

Realizing what a fool she'd been?

Or was she as exhausted as Scout, the grueling three-mile hike taking its toll?

Scout didn't ask. She was afraid to strike up a conversation, afraid of what Eleanor might say and of her response. She didn't get angry often. She didn't ever have much to get angry about, but she'd seen red when Eleanor had said she'd have forgotten Lucy. Every thought in her head had flown out, and all she could feel was rage.

"We're ready," Boone said quietly.

She turned to face him, her pulse jumping with nerves and fear.

"You know what to do, right?" he asked, his hand on her shoulder. "There's no chance he's going to let you leave with Lucy. You're going to have to find a way to get your daughter into another room."

"I'll help," Eleanor said. "I'm sure I can distract him for a few minutes. There's a bathroom at the back of the cabin with a window in it. It's tiny, but I'm sure you and Lucy can squeeze through. The only other window on that side of the house has shades that Gaige keeps closed. He won't be able to see anyone approaching from the back unless he opens them. If you can get into the bathroom, maybe someone can be waiting under the window to grab Lucy."

"What about you?" Scout asked. The woman was a criminal, a kidnapper and a fool, but Scout didn't want her left in the cabin alone with Gaige. Regardless of what Eleanor thought, the man was dangerous. He'd nearly killed Scout, and she doubted he'd hesitated to hurt anyone who got in his way.

"Why do you care?" Eleanor asked.

"Because you're a human being, and I don't want you hurt," Boone said.

"Whatever!" She turned, stalked back to her little shelter under the tree.

Boone ignored her. His gaze was on Scout, his expression soft and unguarded. She could see the worry in his eyes, the anxiety on his face.

"I'll be okay," she said, as much to convince herself as him.

He nodded. "I know."

"Then why do you look worried?"

"Because I care, and because I want to go in there for you, and I can't. Gaige sees me coming and there's no telling what he'll do to Lucy."

"I know."

"Then I guess you know how dangerous this situation is, and I guess you know just how helpless I feel right now." He ground the words out, his eyes flashing with frustration.

He didn't look angry, though. He looked like a man who knew how to love and who deserved to *be* loved, and in that moment, Scout wished she had been brave enough to do more than promise him cake. She wished that she'd been confident enough, strong enough, sure enough of herself to tell him that she wanted there to be an *us* once Lucy was home.

"Boone," she said, wanting to get the words out, because she was afraid there might not be another opportunity to say them.

"Just focus on the mission, Scout," he said quietly, brushing strands of hair from her cheeks, tucking them under her hood. "We'll work everything else out afterward."

"But—"

"Focus. Stay calm. Find a way to get Lucy into that bathroom, and find a way out the window. Okay?" he urged.

She nodded, because her throat was tight with fear and hope and something she wasn't sure she'd ever felt before. Not attraction. Not infatuation. Something deeper, more lasting.

She touched his jaw, her hand sliding over several days' worth of stubble. It felt soft beneath her fingers, and she levered up, her lips brushing his.

He pulled her close, his hands sliding down her arms, his fingers linking with hers. Palm to palm, warmth to warmth, and she knew that if she had a thousand years to stand in Boone's arms, it would never be enough.

He broke away, his forehead pressed to hers.

"That," he rasped, "was the most fun I have ever had breaking a rule. Now go. The longer we put this off, the more antsy Gaige is going to be." He nudged her toward the cabin, and she went, her lips still warm from their kiss.

Eleanor stepped into place beside her. They didn't speak as they approached the cabin. There was nothing to say. The plans had been set; everything had been worked out. In the forest surrounding them, a dozen men and women were watching. Scout should have felt comforted by that, but all she felt was terror.

What if Lucy wasn't in the cabin?

What if Gaige had already left for the airport?

Was it possible he'd got wind of Eleanor's capture?

Did he know he was about to be betrayed?

The questions pounded through her head as they stepped from the canopy of the trees and into an overgrown clearing. The cabin sat in the center of it, a small porch at the front with an old hanging swing worn with age.

Up close, the place had an abandoned feel, and she wondered if he really had left.

The front door swung open, but no one appeared on the threshold.

Did he know that the cabin was being watched?

Eleanor grabbed her arm, long fingernails digging through the parka and her coat. "Remember," she hissed. "The bathroom in the back of the cabin. Take Lucy there. It's the only room with a lock on the door."

"Okay."

"One more thing." She slowed her steps, looked straight into Scout's eyes. "I'm sorry. For all of this. I was played a fool before, and I didn't think I'd ever be played a fool again. Pride goeth before the fall." She laughed, the sound sending chills up Scout's spine.

"What—?"

"Shh." Eleanor cut her off as they stepped onto the porch. Sure enough, a man was standing just beyond the doorway, the shadowy interior of the cabin hiding his face. It couldn't hide the child he was holding, though. Not a dark-haired little girl. A blonde.

For a moment, Scout's heart stopped, every fear she'd had about Lucy not being at the cabin stealing her breath and making her feel dizzy and faint. Or maybe it was the scent of gasoline that was making her feel that way.

Gasoline?

It couldn't be.

Could it? She inhaled, nearly gagging on the fumes. They stung her nose, made her lungs hurt.

She backed up, fear crawling along her nerves, settling like a hard knot in her chest.

Something wasn't right.

She wanted to signal to Boone, let him know that things weren't working out the way they'd planned.

Then she heard something that she'd been afraid she'd

never hear again, the sound as sweet as the first bird-song of spring.

"Mommy! Mommy, let's go home!" Lucy cried, her voice hoarse, her hand reaching out.

Scout didn't hesitate, didn't think another thought about the acrid scent. She ran into the cabin and snatched Lucy from the man's arms.

They were in, the cabin door closing behind Eleanor.

That was Boone's signal to move, and he did, winding his way along the edges of the trees, staying low and hidden by the overgrowth of vegetation until he was at the back of the cabin.

He eyed the building, scanning the one-story log exterior. The window Eleanor had mentioned was there, a small rectangle cut into the wood, its glass wet from the storm. Higher than he'd anticipated, probably close to seven feet up, it barely looked big enough for a child to fit through.

Would Scout be able to squeeze through the opening? She was small, but the opening looked tiny.

The only other window on the back of the building was triple the size. Just as Eleanor had said, the shades were drawn.

Leaves rustled behind him. He didn't bother looking to see who it was. Cyrus had been assigned to the back quadrant of the cabin, and Boone had no doubt he was about to make an appearance.

"You're usually quieter than that." He tossed the words over his shoulder, his attention completely focused on the cabin.

"You usually don't show up in my quadrant." Cyrus slid from the shadow of an elm tree, his movements so smooth that it almost seemed that he wasn't moving at all. "You're supposed to be at the front of the house. Since you're not, I'm assuming something has come up."

"You're assuming right." Boone filled him in quickly, his gaze riveted to the small window. Nothing yet. Not a hint of movement from beyond it.

"Might have been a good idea to fill everyone else in," Cyrus said when Boone finished speaking. There was no heat in his words and no judgment. They trusted each other implicitly, had worked together enough to know that every move was made deliberately, every decision thought through carefully.

"It *would* have been a good idea," Boone corrected. "But I wasn't sure Eleanor was being honest about the window until I got here, and I didn't want to waste time on a last-minute scramble to get back into position."

"The window's there," Cyrus pointed out. "Want me to make the call?"

"Yeah. Thanks. Tell the team that if Scout signals me, we'll need a distraction at the front of the house. I don't want Gaige looking out the window as I'm approaching. I'm not sure how he'll react if he sees me."

"Does he have a weapon?" Cyrus asked, gathering all the facts the way he normally did. He'd spout them back when he radioed the team, and Boone had no doubt he'd get every last detail right.

"Eleanor didn't mention one, but Scout was nearly killed with a .45. I'd say there's a good possibility that he does."

"Got it. So, she signals and we provide a distraction at the front of the building. What if she doesn't signal?"

"Then we move to plan B," Boone responded.

Cyrus didn't ask what that plan was. He'd worked with Boone for too many years to think there was one.

Instead, he slipped deeper into the trees, murmuring something into his radio. They tried to maintain radio silence on missions like these, but with so many entities working together on this rescue, it wasn't possible. That suited Boone fine. He wanted quick communication. If the bathroom window opened, he needed a way to keep Gaige from figuring out that his prisoners were escaping.

Cyrus returned a few seconds later, binoculars in hand, his attention on the back of the cabin. "Any movement at the window?"

"Not yet."

"We've got some stuff going on off scene. FBI found a Gaige Thompson from San Jose. He's a divorce lawyer. Wife says he's on a business trip and won't be home for a couple of weeks."

"She give any indication of where he went?"

"Washington, D.C." Cyrus lowered the binoculars. "Guy is licensed to practice law there and in California. He's pretty well-known in political circles, has helped a lot of high-level people avoid messy divorce battles."

"Nice," Boone said, his gaze still on the cabin. No movement there. Nothing to indicate that Scout had made it into the bathroom.

"Not if he's in that cabin with the kid."

Bam!

Fire exploded from the front of the building, flames leaping into the sky.

Boone sprinted forward, racing to the back of the cabin, praying that the bathroom window would open and Scout would appear. It stayed closed, the glass just above head level.

Too late, his brain shouted. *You're too late. Again.*

His radio buzzed, people calling for ambulance crews and fire trucks. Others yelling for flanking to the left and right of the house. Someone called for a bomb unit, and someone else was calling his name over and over again. Fire blazed and crackled at the front of the cabin. Men and women streamed out of the woods, racing toward the burning building.

He ignored it all.

His focus was on the window and the chance that Scout and Lucy might have made it into the room beyond it.

He dropped his pack onto the ground, stood on it, looking into a room filled with swirling smoke. Nothing. No sign of anyone or anything, but he wasn't ready to give up hope, wasn't ready to stop believing that God would bring Lucy and Scout out of this alive.

No way could he fit through the bathroom window, so he used the pack as a battering ram, slamming it against the other window, glass shattering into a million pieces, smoke billowing out, everything moving in slow motion except for the fire. It crawled up the roof of the cabin with warp speed, consuming wood, melting metal and destroying everything in its path.

SIXTEEN

Lucy was crying.

Scout heard it through a fog of pain.

She opened her eyes, coughing as smoke filled her lungs. "It's okay, Lucy," she tried to say, but a fit of coughing stole the words.

No sound from Lucy, and she almost closed her eyes again, let herself drift away from the pain. Above her, thick black smoke swirled near the ceiling, but she felt no sense of urgency, no need to get up and find a way out.

Somewhere close by, a child coughed, the sound just enough to make Scout turn her head. Lucy lay beside her, limp as a rag doll. At least, she thought it was Lucy. The hair was blond, not brown.

It didn't matter. Whoever the little girl was, she was in trouble, and Scout had to help her.

She managed to get to her knees, blood dripping from her head, memories flooding back. Short, stocky Gaige with his bright blue eyes and cocky smile. Eleanor. Their argument over whether or not Lucy was going to go to the airport with them. Eleanor meeting Scout's eyes, something in her gaze warning her that she needed to find a way out.

Lucy had already been in Scout's arms, clinging to her and begging to go home. Scout had backed down a hall and found her way into a tiny bathroom, closing and locking the door. She set Lucy in the shower stall and climbed on the toilet seat.

And... What?

She couldn't remember anything else, but somehow she'd ended up on the floor with smoke everywhere.

She coughed again, lifting Lucy into her arms. She didn't have time to grab a towel and soak it. The door was intact, but hot to the touch. There was no escape that way. She climbed onto the toilet, the window within reach. Her fingers were clumsy as she tried to unlock it one-handed. The latch moved, but the window wouldn't open.

She needed to put Lucy down, but she was afraid that if she did, she'd never find her again.

Please, God, she prayed. *Please help me save my daughter.*

She slammed her hand against the glass, but her movements were sluggish, the smoke stealing every bit of oxygen in the room. She tried again, her muscles so weak she could barely slap the glass.

Something banged on the other side of her hand, and the glass shattered, falling like rain all around her, the smoke pouring up and out into gray daylight.

Hands reached in, and a voice shouted for her to hand Lucy out. She struggled to do as she'd been asked, the fire lapping at the door, crawling toward her across the floor.

And suddenly, Lucy was out, and Scout was alone in the room, the heat of the flames searing her skin, her head swimming with the need to give in, let go, allow herself to give up.

"Don't you dare give up now!" Boone shouted, reaching into the window, his hand brushing her face. "Come on, Scout! You've got to help me. This window is too narrow. My shoulders won't fit through. I can't come in. You've got to come to me," he said, and there was so much desperation in his voice, she made herself grab the windowsill, broken glass slicing into her palms as she tried to lever into the opening.

He grabbed her arms, yanked her through, icy rain falling on her heated skin, cold air filling her lungs as Boone carried her to the edge of the clearing. He stopped there, lowered her onto the ground, pulling off his coat and covering her with it.

A few feet away, a man held Lucy, her body so limp and fragile Scout's heart shattered into a million pieces.

"Is she dead?" she wanted to say, but all she could do was cough, her lungs burning and heaving, her mind screaming as Cyrus laid Lucy on the ground, his palm pressing against her chest as he tried to force her heart to beat again.

No! She wanted to shout, because they'd come so far, worked so hard to bring her baby home. She tried to sit up, tried to run to her little girl, but Boone pressed her back down, said something to someone she couldn't see.

Jackson edged in next to him, kneeling beside Scout, blocking her view of Cyrus. She saw Boone's red hair and his shoulders behind Jackson, knew he had gone to help.

"Move!" she rasped, shoving against Jackson without any force, because she had no strength.

"You're injured. You can't help your daughter if you

don't help yourself." Jackson pressed something to her head, and she brushed it away and sat up, pushing at his hands with every bit of power she had left.

She was on her knees, then her feet, ignoring his command to stay down, stumbling to her daughter's side.

"Lucy," she croaked, dropping down beside Boone, darkness clouding the edges of her vision as she watched him breathe for her daughter.

SEVENTEEN

"Come on! Breathe!" Boone muttered, every bit of the desperation he felt seeping into the words.

"Breathe!" he said again as Cyrus compressed her chest.

"Thirty!" he called, and Boone breathed into her mouth.

Once. Twice.

Lucy coughed, her eyes fluttering open, deep brown and filled with confusion. She tried to cry, her mouth opening, nothing but gasping coughs escaping.

He touched her head, smoothed her soot-stained hair, his heart beating frantically. They'd almost lost her.

Had lost her.

He'd felt the limpness of her body as he'd lifted her from Scout's arms, and he'd known that she was gone, had prayed as he'd handed her to Cyrus, begged God to give her back to Scout. "It's okay, sweetie. You're okay."

She wasn't.

Her respiration was shallow, her heartbeat thready. They needed to get her to a hospital. The sooner the better.

"We need an oxygen mask," Cyrus hollered, the relief on his face raw and real. He'd been through this before, years ago, and as far as Boone knew, he'd never got over it.

Lucy coughed again and again, and Boone rubbed her chest and stomach, terrified she'd stop breathing.

"Lucy!" Scout leaned in, trying to lift her daughter from the ground, tears streaming down her face. He wasn't sure if they were tears of relief or fear, but they left streaks in the soot that covered her cheeks.

"Shh," Boone said. "You're going to scare her more than she already is."

She nodded, but the tears kept rolling down her face, and Lucy's harsh, raspy coughs continued.

He lifted the little girl, set her in Scout's lap, his heart beating hollowly in his chest. Both were covered in soot and breathing rapidly, their respirations shallow. A few more minutes and they would have succumbed to smoke inhalation. He'd almost lost them, and he couldn't shake the thought that he still could.

An ATV pulled up beside them, an EMT jumping off and running to Scout's side. Five minutes later, she and Lucy were en route to the lodge, where an ambulance was waiting to transport them to the hospital. The cabin fire had nearly been doused by a team of forest rangers, and Boone was staring at the smoldering ruin, his heart still beating too hard and fast in his chest, his mind going back to that moment when he'd realized how futile his rescue attempt was. Flames had been shooting out the bedroom window, and he'd been trying desperately to get past them.

If Cyrus hadn't pulled him away, he'd have probably found a way. And then what?

Would he have made it into the bathroom?

"You're a mess, Anderson," Jackson said, his tone much more solemn than usual. "Maybe Lucy and Scout aren't the only ones who need a trip to the hospital."

"I'm fine," he growled.

"You're angry," Jackson retorted. "You think you could have done something different, affected a different outcome."

"I could have broken the bathroom window before I tried to get in another way. I could have got them both out sooner. Then maybe they wouldn't be in such bad shape."

"You're giving yourself way too much credit," Jackson cut in.

"What's that supposed to mean?"

"You think that you get to decide who lives and dies. That by your actions a life is saved or not."

"No," he argued. "I don't. I think that I have a responsibility to do my best. I think that if I have an opportunity to help, I'm obligated to do it."

"If that's really what you think, then why are you beating yourself up over this? Scout and Lucy are both alive, and they're both going to be fine. What more can you ask of yourself?"

"A lot," he ground out. "That little girl was dead, Jackson. When I took her from Scout, she was gone." His voice broke, and he had to swallow hard to keep tears from falling. "If I'd been there a few minutes sooner—"

"If you'd been there a few minutes *later,* there wouldn't have been any chance of resuscitating her. Much as I hate to make your big head any bigger—" Jackson ran a hand over his hair and sighed "—you did good. Don't play the what-if game on this one, Boone. Just be thankful that things worked out the way they did."

"I am thankful. I just wish—"

"Right. Wish. Hope. Want. So, here you are, standing there regretting something that didn't even happen while Scout and Lucy are heading to the hospital without you."

"Was I supposed to hang off the back of the ATV?"

"No, but you could be walking out of here instead of feeling sorry for yourself."

"I am not," he growled, "feeling sorry for myself. There are things to do around here. Lamar and Rodriguez are going to want a rundown of everything Eleanor said and did on the way here." He glanced at the burned-out shell of the cabin. The entire front was gone, the eaves of the porch caved in. "It doesn't look like she had any chance of escaping. I didn't much like the lady, but she didn't deserve that."

"I don't guess she did," Jackson agreed. "Something accelerated the blaze. Makes me wonder if that was the kidnapper's plan all along. Get rid of everyone and leave town. Go back to his family and pretend nothing had ever happened."

"In other words, all he wanted was the information written on the photo."

"Seems to me that might be the case," Jackson responded. "Stella called in a few minutes ago. She met Christopher Schoepflin at the airport, and she asked him if he knew Gaige Thompson."

"Let me guess. Thompson represented his father during his divorces."

"Exactly."

"What a mess," Boone muttered.

"Yeah. It is, and it's going to take a while to sort out. I'm thinking that you might want to head to the hospital before you're dragged downtown to answer a bunch of questions."

"Are you telling me to leave the scene?"

"That's exactly what I'm telling you. Get Cyrus and take off. Go to the hospital, because I can guarantee you that when Scout looks for someone who will tell her that her daughter is going to be okay, it's you she's going to be looking for. If you get dragged to the sheriff's office, it's going to be hours before you can be there for her."

"You're being awfully accommodating, Jackson," Boone said, but he grabbed his backpack, shook shards of glass off of it and put it on.

"Aren't I always?"

"No."

Jackson shrugged. "Hey, if you're not interested in the job, I'm sure Cyrus would be willing to hold Scout's hand while she waits for news. Of course, you know how bad his bedside manners are."

Boone knew. Cyrus had sat vigil at the hospital when Boone had been recovering from his fractured skull. It hadn't been pleasant for either of them.

"You'll call me when you have any news? Scout will want to be updated."

"I'll call or stop by the hospital. I don't know how much more they can do here. They won't be able to recover Eleanor's or Gaige's body until what's left of the structure is stabilized. It could be days before they know how the fire started. Like I said, there's no sense in waiting around while they do their job. I'm going to talk to Lamar, and then I'm heading back to town. Since you'll have good cell phone reception, why don't you give Chance a call when you get back to town? Let him know what's going on."

There it was. The reason Jackson was pushing Boone to leave. "I should have known you had ulterior motives. You don't want to be the one to tell your brother that we were around this much chaos, so you're passing the job on to me."

"I don't mind telling him. I just prefer not to listen to his response," Jackson said with a smile. "I'm going to find Lamar. You get Cyrus and get out of here." He gave him a none-too-gentle shove in the right direction and walked away.

Boone didn't need to be told twice. Not when doing what he was told meant being near Scout.

Scout needed to see her daughter. She didn't care what the doctor said about needing to rest, didn't care what the nurses told her about being weak and unsteady on her feet, didn't care about anything but making sure Lucy was okay.

She struggled out of the bed they'd put her in, tossed the blanket around her shoulders and dragged her IV pole into the hall. There was an elevator sign to the left, and she headed in that direction.

Lucy was in the pediatric ICU, and she was stable.

That was the extent of the information Scout had received, and it didn't touch on whether or not Lucy was awake, unconscious, crying, calm. Scout needed to know those things with a desperation that pounded through her aching head, refused to allow her to close her eyes or rest.

She punched the elevator button, waiting impatiently

for it to open. As soon as it did, she walked on, bumping into a man who was heading out.

"Sorry," she began, looking up into a face that made her heart melt and her legs go weak.

"Boone," she managed to say as he opened his arms.

She stepped into his embrace, her arms winding around his waist, her head settling against his chest.

He smelled like smoke and rain, and she burrowed closer, her hands fisting in his shirt. It didn't matter that Cyrus was watching or that a nurse had made her way to the elevator and was loudly explaining why Scout couldn't leave the floor.

Boone was there, and she felt down deep in her soul that everything was going to be okay.

"Going somewhere?" he asked, smoothing her hair back, frowning at the fresh bandage on her forehead. "Because from the look of things, you should probably be in bed."

"I want to see Lucy."

"And you *will* see her, Scout," the nurse said, holding the elevator doors open. "After you're both feeling a little better."

"I think," Boone said, "that it would be difficult for any mother to feel good when her child is injured. If you want them both to heal and get better, you should have them together."

"We're doing this in the best interest of both of them," the nurse responded sincerely. "We understand the extenuating circumstances and that the two have been separated for several days, but the doctor is worried that too much excitement might contribute to respiratory distress. Especially in Lucy. The next thirty-six hours are critical."

"I can see the doctor's point," Cyrus cut in. "How about we all just be reasonable about this?"

"What are you talking about?" Scout demanded, because she wasn't in the mood to be reasonable.

"Let him do his thing," Boone whispered in her ear, his breath tickling against her skin and lodging somewhere deep in her heart.

"What I'm talking about," Cyrus responded, stepping off the elevator and walking a few feet away, "is all of us being where we need to be and doing what we need to do. We wouldn't want to break any hospital rules."

"It's not about rules." The nurse turned to face him, her hand slipping from the elevator door. "It's about doing what is best for our—"

The door slid closed, cutting off whatever she was going to say.

"There," Boone said with a half smile. "Cyrus at his finest. Now, I don't suppose you have any idea where they're keeping Lucy?"

"Pediatric ICU," she responded. "But I have no idea where that is."

"Fortunately for you, I do. Samuel had a pretty bad infection a few months ago, and they kept him in the ICU overnight." He punched a button, his free arm around her waist, his fingers warm through the cotton hospital gown. She could feel his palm through the fabric, feel his breath ruffling her hair, feel the heat of his body seeping through the blanket and gown, and she wanted to lean into him, close her eyes, just let herself relax against his strength.

She shivered with emotions she hadn't expected to feel, and he tucked the blanket closer around her, his fingers sliding along her neck, brushing against the tender skin there. "Cold?"

"Scared," she admitted.

"Lucy is going to be okay."

"I'm worried for her, but that's not why I'm scared."

"Then what?" he asked as the elevator door opened.

"You. Us. The things you were talking about at the ski resort," she admitted. She couldn't hide things from Boone. Not after what he'd done for her and for Lucy. Not after she'd looked deep into his eyes, tasted his lips, spent days knowing that he was the one person who understood her grief and pain.

"That," he said, his hand cupping her elbow as he led her to the pediatric ICU, "is not something to be afraid of."

"That's easy for you to say. You haven't made the mistakes I have."

"Maybe not, but I've made plenty of other ones. I've trusted and loved someone who wasn't trustworthy. I've spent too much time away from people I cared about and lost my daughter because of it. I've failed again and again, Scout." He stopped, turned so they were facing each other. "And every single time, God has picked me up and brushed me off and let me have another chance. This is your chance. *I'm* your chance. And you know what? You're mine."

"Boone…" She had a dozen things she wanted to say, but none of them seemed right, because not one of them could match the pure and simple honesty of his words. "I don't know what to say to that."

"You don't have to say anything. You just have to tell me the truth. Are you going to walk away from us because you might fail again? If you are, I need to know it now rather than a year from now."

"I'm not," she said. Simply. Honestly. Because he deserved it.

A slow smile spread across his face, tension easing from his jaw and his shoulders. "You're sure? Because I've got a crazy life, Scout, and I can't give it up. I'm away for days and weeks at a time. When I'm home, I'm tired and—"

"Hungry?" she suggested, and he chuckled.

"I am always hungry," he said. "But when I get back from a mission, I'm tired and worn, and sometimes, I'm a little quiet and a lot grumpy. That's not going to be easy to deal with."

"But it's going to be worth it," she assured him. "Because you are everything I didn't know I needed—everything I never knew I wanted. You really are my second chance, Boone. And I'm not going to turn my back on that—or you."

"We'll see if you're still saying that in twenty years," he quipped, pushing open double-wide doors that led into the ICU reception area.

"At the end of a lifetime, I will still be saying it," she assured him.

"I hope so," he said.

"I *believe* so," she responded. "There's a difference."

He shook his head, that easy smile that she loved so much curving the edges of his mouth. "You're throwing my words back in my face. Do you plan to do that often?"

"Yes."

He laughed, dropping a quick kiss to her lips, a lifetime of promises in his eyes, in the gentleness of his touch.

"Glad to hear it, Scout, because I'm planning to say a lot of really wonderful things to you in the future. Come on. Let's go see your daughter."

He took her hand and they walked to Lucy's side together.

EIGHTEEN

Apparently, children recovered from nearly dying much more quickly than adults did.

The thought flitted through Scout's mind as she watched Lucy twirl around the living room, her nightgown swirling around her legs. Nearly four weeks after the fire and she didn't seem any worse for wear. Cheeks pink, newly cropped hair bouncing in short brown ringlets around her head, she giggled and danced and acted for all the world as if they'd never been apart.

If it hadn't been one in the morning, that would have been great, but it was, and Scout was exhausted.

The past few weeks had been…challenging.

She'd had to face Christopher and Rachel, explain the circumstances of Lucy's birth, ask for forgiveness for the secret she'd kept. They'd been gracious and kind, but it had still been hard. She'd kept Christopher from his daughter for nearly three years, and no matter how much she'd justified it in her mind, no matter how scared she'd been, she hadn't had the right to do it.

Somehow, Christopher had understood. He'd listened as she'd explained Amber's words and her warning, and he'd said that he'd have made the same decision she had.

She wasn't sure it was true, but she'd been grateful. When he'd asked for twice-yearly visits with Lucy, Scout had been happy to comply.

For now, things were going the way they had before the kidnapping. Aside from a quick visit while Lucy was in the hospital, Christopher had stayed away. He and his father were dealing with a firestorm of media attention as the FBI investigated Christopher and Amber's stepmother, Alaina.

Special Agent Rodriguez had confirmed that the FBI had found information hidden at the crypt where Scout's parents were buried. Rolled up and wrapped in cellophane, the three small pieces of paper had been hidden in a vase attached to the wall. Scrawled on each was the name of a bank and the number of a safe-deposit box. Each box had been filled with photos of women, interviews with them, long pages of stories about how they'd been tricked into traveling to the United States for job opportunities, sold to the highest bidder and made to work for nearly nothing.

If the FBI was right, Amber had been working on an exposé that would reveal her stepmother's involvement in what amounted to a modern-day slave trade.

It didn't surprise Scout. As much as Amber loved to party, she also loved social justice. She always rooted for the underdog and cheered for the dark horse.

She'd have been excited to expose Alaina's illegal business and reroute the millions of dollars that she claimed Alaina made from it into social reform. Maybe she'd got in too deep, or maybe she'd found something even more incendiary than what had been found in the safe-deposit boxes. Whatever the case, the FBI believed she'd been worried about how deep she was digging, that she'd been afraid for her life.

Rather than going to the authorities, she'd done what Amber always did—pushed harder, dug deeper, done everything she could to keep the party going for as long as she could. Special Agent Rodriguez speculated that Amber had told her stepmother about the hidden information in a last-ditch effort to stay alive.

It hadn't worked. Alaina had murdered Amber or hired someone to do it. According to Agent Rodriguez, a small storage unit that Amber had secretly rented had been auctioned off at the beginning of November, and a box of her personal belongings had been discovered and returned to the Schoepflin family. Several diaries were in the box. Most of the information in them was mundane, but there was mention of the letters and gifts Amber had sent to Scout highlighted in pink. Agent Rodriguez believed that had been enough to worry Alaina.

Alaina wasn't admitting to it, and with Gaige Thompson dead, they couldn't question him, but it seemed that had been the catalyst to everything else that had happened.

The two had been friends for years. Such close friends that they'd traveled together with their spouses, had Christmas and Thanksgiving meals together. Dale Schoepflin was cooperating fully with the investigation, and he claimed that both he and his wife had known about Gaige's relationship with Eleanor. He said that it had begun shortly before Scout left San Jose.

Unlike his son, he'd known about Scout's pregnancy. He'd overheard Amber discussing it with her, knew that Amber had told Scout to leave town. He and Alaina had both suspected that the child was Christopher's, and they'd decided to make moving away easy for Scout. They'd asked Gaige to find her a job opportunity and an inexpensive rental in a nice neighborhood. Gaige had met Eleanor while he was in River Valley, opening doors that probably would have stayed closed for Scout if not for the Schoepflin family.

She shivered.

She'd spent years afraid of being found, and she'd never really been hidden.

Scout walked to the Christmas tree she'd set up in the corner of the living room. With Eleanor dead, the fate of her little house was up in the air. Next year, Scout and Lucy might be somewhere else. Maybe it would be for the best. Even with the little tree decorated with tinsel and Christmas lights, the house didn't feel like home. Not like it used to.

Funny how that didn't matter as much as it used to.

Lucy zipped past, reaching for the sparkly pink frame that hung from the tree.

"Pretty, Mommy," she said.

"It is," she responded, her throat tight with hundreds of memories of Amber as a child and a teenager and an adult. She missed her friend, but she saw hints of her in Lucy's face.

Lucy reached for another frame. Hand carved from pinewood, it held a photo of Scout, Boone and Lucy, sitting at a booth in a diner on Main Street. Scout had just got her staples out, and Boone had taken them to lunch to celebrate. He'd asked the waitress to snap the photo, and Scout's cheeks had been pink with embarrassment. In the photo, she'd been looking at him, and he'd been looking at Lucy, and the love they all had for each other nearly jumped out of the frame.

She missed Boone more than she wanted to let herself admit.

He'd been on a mission for a week, gone somewhere that he couldn't talk about, doing things he couldn't explain. He'd given her the frame the night before he'd left, told her to put another picture inside. One that didn't have his ugly mug in it.

He must have known that she wouldn't do it.

He must have known that she would walk to the frame every other minute of every day just to see him smiling that soft easy smile of his.

"Boone! I want Boone," Lucy cried.

"He'll visit as soon as he finishes his job."

"When?" Lucy asked, her little hands on her hips, her lower lip out. She hadn't been sleeping well since the kidnapping. She did well at day care and fine while the sun was out, but as soon as bedtime rolled around, she tossed and turned, woke crying, sobbed about things living under the bed and in the closet. The sleepless nights were taking a toll on both of them, but with Christmas just around the corner, Scout was trying to be cheerful.

"I don't know when he'll be back, but I'm hoping it will be soon." Boone hadn't been able to give her anything more than a vague time frame. A week. Maybe two. If he was going to be longer, he'd promised that someone from HEART would contact her.

"I want Boone!" Lucy insisted, and Scout picked her up, snuggling her close, inhaling the sweet smell of baby shampoo and lotion.

"Me, too, but he's not here."

"Tomorrow?"

"Maybe."

"Mommy," Lucy said, pressing her palms to Scout's cheeks. "I want cake."

The request made Scout chuckle. "Not at this time of the morning."

"We have cake for Boone."

True. She'd made a different flavor cake every day that Boone was in town. Thinking about how much he'd enjoyed each flavor and each kind of frosting made her smile.

"Tell you what," she said, glancing out the window at the dark morning and gray-blue clouds that drifted lazily across the moon. Somewhere, it was full light, and somewhere Boone was working hard to reunite another family. "Let's make cake."

"Cake!" Lucy squealed with glee, running into the kitchen ahead of her.

They took out the bowls and the hand mixer, the eggs and the flour. Scout had never made a coconut cake for Boone, but she thought he'd like her grandmother's recipe.

It didn't take long to mix the batter, and soon the scent of vanilla and coconut filled the air. They spent two hours baking and frosting the cake. It was still dark when they finished. Outside, the first snowflakes of the season drifted lazily from the sky.

"Look," Scout said, lifting Lucy so she could see out the window over the sink. "It's snowing."

"Let's go play," Lucy mumbled, half-asleep, the adventure of being awake and baking cake before the sun came up finally wearing her down.

"Not yet. We'll wait until the sun rises."

"And Boone comes?"

"Sure," she said, because she had to trust that he

would come. That wherever he was, God would bring him back to them.

She carried Lucy into the living room, laying her down on the new love seat and covering her with a throw. She turned off the lamp, plugged in the Christmas-tree lights so that they twinkled multicolored in the darkness.

She thought about turning on some Christmas music, letting the quiet sounds of it soothe her to sleep, but she didn't bother, just lay on the couch watching the snow fall on the front yard, praying that wherever Boone was, he was safe.

Headlights flashed on the newly fallen snow, splashing over her driveway and across the shrubs and trees that lined it.

Surprised, she stood, walking to the window and watching as a car rolled along the driveway.

No. Not a car.

She pressed her face close to the glass, her heart jumping. An SUV.

Boone!

She was out the door and across the yard before he parked, throwing herself into his arms as he stepped out of the vehicle.

"You're back," she cried, and he kissed the sound from her lips, kissed her forehead, her cheek.

"You smell like cake," he whispered in her ear, and she laughed through tears that shouldn't have been falling.

"Lucy and I were awake. She insisted we have cake."

"Is there any left?" he asked, his arm sliding around her waist, his hands strumming along her sides. He seemed thinner, his face shadowed by a beard that hadn't been there when he left.

"Plenty."

"Good, because Stella and Cyrus are with me, and they're not happy."

"And cake isn't going to make us happy," Stella grumbled as she climbed out of the SUV. "You don't shanghai someone and then think they're going to be pleasant."

"I don't mind being shanghaied as long as there's a bed on the other end of the trip." Cyrus got out and stretched, his body leaner than it had been the last time she'd seen him.

Had he been ill?

She didn't ask, just led the way into the house while Stella mumbled about bringing her own car to the airport the next time they went on a mission together.

"Shh," Cyrus said as he walked into the house. "The kid is asleep, and that's exactly what I want to be, too. You got a place I can bed down, Scout?"

"Lucy's room. It's down the hall. The first room on the ri—"

He was already gone, Stella following along behind him, shooting Boone a hard look as she went.

"She's not happy," Scout said, and Boone shrugged.

"She'll get over it."

"What'd you do?"

"Refused to bring her home. She wanted me to bring her into D.C. I wanted to come here. Since it was snowing, I was afraid I might not make it if I took a side trip."

"I would have been here when you *did* make it."

"I don't know if I would have survived that long."

"Without cake?" she joked, and he shook his head.

"Without you and Lucy. I missed you, babe. More than I can say. There was a moment when I was gone that all I could do was pray that God was going to bring me home to you."

"He did." She led him into the kitchen, pressed him down into a chair. "He will. Always. I have to believe that or I won't be able to live my life while you're gone."

He smiled, taking a cup of coffee that she handed him and setting it on the table.

She put a slice of coconut cake down in front of him, but he didn't touch it, just grabbed her hand, pulling her close. "How is Lucy?"

"Ornery. She doesn't sleep well. It shows."

"Time will heal that." He stood and they were inches apart. She could see the dark circles under his eyes, the pale cast to his skin. He looked tired and a little sad, and her heart ached for him.

She wrapped her arms around his waist, hugging him tight because she didn't know what else to do. "Are you okay?"

"I will be. After a few long walks in the snow with the woman I love. Did you put a new photo in the frame?"

"And miss out on seeing your ugly mug every day?" she joked, wanting to ease some of the sadness from his eyes.

He didn't laugh, just studied her face intently. "Then you missed out."

"On what?"

"My secret message." He led her into the living room, handed her the frame. "Go ahead. Open it up."

Her fingers shook as she slid the back clasps open and lifted the back of the frame. There, on the back of the photo, were letters and numbers.

D.B.A.

S.C.

L.C.
Together 4 ever?
She met his eyes, her heart pounding wildly.

"Boone—"

"I love you, Scout. I love your daughter. I don't want to come home from a mission, go back to my empty apartment and wait until a decent hour to visit or call you. I don't want to barge in on your life at four in the morning and have to leave a few hours later, because I have no right to stay."

"You have every right to stay." She touched his cheeks, slid her hands to his shoulders, feeling all the tension that he'd carried on his trip and wanting desperately to take it away. "I can always make space for you and your team."

"I am not my team," he responded. "Not when I'm here. Here, I am just me, and I want to come home to you and to Lucy. I want to know, when I'm crawling through mud and blood and searching for people that I don't know and have never met, that when I come home, I'm returning to my family."

"And I want to know when you're gone," she responded softly, "that family is exactly what you'll be returning to."

He smiled then, leaning down, kissing her so gently, her heart ached with it.

"My world is right again," he said quietly, and it was as if those words freed something in him, some of the old Boone peeking out from the depth of his eyes.

"Mine, too," Scout whispered, kissing him again, holding him tight, trying to will the peace that he deserved into his tired body.

He broke away, his eyes dark with longing, his lips curving in that sweet, sweet smile. "Better stop, Scout, because I don't think there's a preacher who'd be willing to marry us at this time of the morning. Seeing as how that's the case, there's only one thing to do."

"What's that?" she asked, and he grabbed her hand, smiled into her eyes.

"Dig into that cake you made," he responded, and she laughed as he tugged her back into the kitchen.

* * * * *

Dear Reader,

Everyone makes mistakes. Sometimes those mistakes change nothing. Sometimes they change everything. For Scout Cramer, one mistake has caused her to lose her home, her job and her friendships. It has also given her the greatest blessing she has ever received. When her young daughter is kidnapped, she will do anything to bring her home safely. With the help of HEART member Boone Anderson, Scout embarks on a desperate hunt that challenges her faith and forces her to look at a past she thought she left far behind. The journey is a difficult one, but through it Scout learns that the most difficult struggles often bring the greatest reward.

I hope you enjoyed this second installment in the Mission: Rescue series! And I hope that as you read it, you were reminded that our pasts do not define us. In the midst of our greatest failures, God reaches down, pulls us up and offers redemption, forgiveness and love.

I love hearing from readers. If you have time, drop me a line at shirlee@shirleemccoy.com.

Blessings,

Shirlee McCoy

Questions for Discussion

1. How are Boone's struggles and Scout's similar? Aside from wanting their daughters back safely, what is it that they both long for?

2. Scout made a mistake that completely changed her life. Are you sympathetic to that mistake? Why or why not?

3. While God's forgiveness is most important, is there a valid reason for thinking that we must also be willing to forgive ourselves? Why is forgiving ourselves sometimes more difficult than forgiving others?

4. Do you have things in your past that are still impacting your life? If so, what steps do you think are necessary to let go and move on?

5. Boone carries around guilt because of what happened with his wife and daughter. Do you think his guilt is justified? Are there things Boone could have done differently that would have led to a different outcome?

6. Amber is an interesting character. She is a wild child with a heart of gold. Why is it that she and Scout became such good friends?

7. What led to Amber's death? Do you think that her actions were foolish? Explain.

8. Do you see Scout as a weak or strong character? Explain.

9. Neither Scout nor Boone is looking for love. Why is it that they fall for each other?

REQUEST YOUR FREE BOOKS!

2 FREE RIVETING INSPIRATIONAL NOVELS
PLUS 2 FREE MYSTERY GIFTS

Love Inspired®
SUSPENSE

SPECIAL EXCERPT FROM

Love Inspired.
SUSPENSE

*SWAT team member Isaac Morrison didn't plan to
fall for his best friend's sister. But when Leah Nichols
and her son are in trouble, he'll stop at nothing to
keep them out of harm's way.*

Read on for a sneak peek of
UNDER THE LAWMAN'S PROTECTION
by Laura Scott

"Stay down. I'm going to go make sure there isn't someone out there."

"Wait!" Leah cried as Isaac was about to open his car
door. "Don't go. Stay here with us."

He was torn between two impossible choices. If someone had shot out the tires on purpose, he couldn't just
wait for that person to come finish them off. Nor did he
want to leave Leah and Ben here alone.

So far he wasn't doing the greatest job of keeping
Hawk's sister and her son safe. If he'd been wearing his
bulletproof gear he would be in better shape to go out to
investigate.

Isaac peered out the window, trying to see if anyone
was out there. Sitting here was making him crazy, so he
decided doing something was better than nothing.

"I'm armed, Leah, so don't worry about me. I promise
I'll do whatever it takes to keep you and Ben safe."

He could tell she wanted to protest, but she bit her lip
and nodded. She pulled her son out of his booster seat

and tucked him next to her so that he was protected on either side. Then she curled her body around him. The fact that she would risk herself to protect Ben gave Isaac a funny feeling in the center of his chest.

Leah's actions were humbling. He hadn't been attracted to a woman in a long time, not since his wife had left him.

But this wasn't the time to ruminate over the past. Isaac's ex-wife and son were gone, and nothing in the world would bring them back. So Isaac would do the next best thing—protect Leah and Ben with his life if necessary.

Don't miss
UNDER THE LAWMAN'S PROTECTION
by Laura Scott,
available January 2015 wherever
Love Inspired® Suspense books and ebooks are sold.

LISEXP1214

Love Inspired

JUST CAN'T GET ENOUGH OF INSPIRATIONAL ROMANCE?

Join our social communities
and talk to us online!
You will have access to the latest
news on upcoming titles and special
promotions, but most important,
you can talk to other fans about your
favorite Love Inspired® reads.

LISOCIAL